REBECCA OF SUNNYBROOK FARM

REBECCA OF SUNNYBROOK FARM

The Woman

Eric Wiggin

Illustrated by Joe Boddy

Wolgemuth & Hyatt, Publishers, Inc.
Brentwood, Tennessee

The mission of Wolgemuth & Hyatt, Publishers, Inc. is to publish and distribute books that lead individuals toward:

- A personal faith in the one true God: Father, Son, and Holy Spirit;
- A lifestyle of practical discipleship; and
- A worldview that is consistent with the historic, Christian faith.

Moreover, the company endeavors to accomplish this mission at a reasonable profit and in a manner which glorifies God and serves His Kingdom.

Published May 1991. First Edition.
Printed in the United States of America.
97 96 95 94 93 92 91   8 7 6 5 4 3 2 1

Wolgemuth & Hyatt, Publishers, Inc.
1749 Mallory Lane, Suite 110
Brentwood, Tennessee 37027

Library of Congress Cataloging-in-Publication Data

Wiggin, Eric E.
Rebecca of Sunnybrook Farm—the woman : a sequel / Eric E. Wiggin. —1st ed.
p. cm.
Summary: At seventeen, Rebecca inherits her Aunt Miranda's estate, and she has high hopes of turning it into a working farm, taking care of her large family, and getting to know railroad executive Adam Ladd even better.
ISBN 1-56121-013-7
[1. New England—Fiction.] I. Wiggin, Kate Douglas Smite, 1856–1923. Rebecca of Sunnybrooke Farm. II. Title.
PZ7.W6376Rg 1991
[Fic]—dc20 91-7907
CIP
AC

To my eldest sons, Mark and Andrew,
who furnished me with models
for Rebecca's brothers, John and Mark,
and
to my youngest son, Bradstreet,
who is anxiously waiting
for his dad's book to get off the press.

CONTENTS

ACKNOWLEDGMENTS

Credit is given to Kate Douglas Wiggin for portions of chapters three and four, which were adapted from her 1906 book, *New Chronicles of Rebecca,* and for her earlier (1903) work, *Rebecca of Sunnybrook Farm,* which inspired the present volume as a sequel.

1

REBECCA'S GREAT EXPECTATIONS

Rebecca Randall drew her sweater tighter over her cotton apron and long housedress against the New England fall chill as she sat on the granite steps of the brick house. The sweater, a scratchy angora and mohair creation, had been Aunt Miranda's. *How like Aunt Miranda herself,* Rebecca thought. *Rough on the outside, yet sturdy, tough, warm all the way through when the occasion called for it.* She flipped her nearly waist-length single black braid across one shoulder, and discovering that the bow she had tied on it earlier was missing, tied it up with a piece of yarn from her pocket and tossed it again behind her. Her dark eyes glistened, moist with tears, yet rimmed with delight as she thought on her past and considered her hopeful future. In all her nearly eighteen years, Rebecca had not imagined a glimpse of these great expectations.

In the days since Rebecca had left dear Sunnybrook Farm to attend Aunt Miranda's funeral and settle affairs at the brick house in Riverboro, her thoughts had often been with her mother, Aurelia Randall, and the children on the farm outside Temperance, Maine. Mother would soon recuperate from her fall from the barn's haymow enough to travel, Rebecca hoped. But for Mother to spend the coming winter months at Sunnybrook was unthinkable. There were Mother and young Fanny to care for, Rebecca knew. There was the house to keep, meals to prepare, cattle to milk, chickens to tend, and firewood to cut at Sunnybrook. *How wonderful,* thought Rebecca, *if they could all be together at the brick house for Christmas!* Mother, however, had not yet replied to Rebecca's letter sent five days earlier suggesting that she and the four children join Rebecca and Aunt Jane in Riverboro.

Rebecca mused on these things—Aunt Miranda's passing, the will in which the brick house was given to her, and the troubling thought that Mother might simply refuse to sell the cattle and pack and leave her home of nearly twenty years. Troubling, too, was the thought of how she would ever feed such a family. Realistically, the farm would not sell until spring, when farmers sought more fields to plant, more land for pasture.

It is true that it had been rumored that Adam's railroad was still interested in purchasing Sunnybrook, and Rebecca had seen surveyors on the farm. But she put the possibility of such a sale out of her mind as the idle speculations of village gossips. Perhaps they would want to buy a right of way across Sunnybrook Farm, but would this even pay off the mortgage—and an iron horse chasing across Sunnybrook's fields might diminish their value to potential purchasers, Rebecca worried.

The proceeds from the sale of Sunnybrook's cattle, fine as they were, would scarcely pay the monthly mortgage bill during the winter months while the farm remained unsold. With no cream, no butter, no eggs to sell, Aurelia Randall's small fortune would quickly dwindle—she might lose Sunnybrook to the bank before it could

A chestnut stallion appeared . . . behind it a new top buggy.

even be sold. Rebecca's bliss turned to fear as she considered that there was not now even a teaching position in Riverboro to bring her a few dollars weekly, and the other jobs she had been offered upon her graduation from Wareham Academy the previous spring had also been filled, she knew.

Now she cast her eyes eastward, toward the plank bridge spanning the rushing Saco River on the road that leads to Maplewood. Many a time during her seven years since coming to the brick house Rebecca had stood on that bridge above the swirling currents. As she had breathed her prayers to God, her sorrows, like the troubled waters beneath her feet, seemed to sweep downstream to disappear in the distant Atlantic.

Rebecca's ears now caught the clatter of hooves and the rattle of wheels on the planks. *The steed drawing this conveyance,* she told herself decidedly, *had been rented from the livery stable in Maplewood. None of the plodding mares or heavy workhorses of Riverboro would trot as quick as that.*

A chestnut stallion appeared at the west end of the bridge, and behind it a new top buggy, its shiny black paint and nickel-plated brass trim strikingly setting off the wheels, gleaming with fresh varnish. The driver was a tall, handsome young man in a natty gray flannel suit, his slate felt fedora cocked jauntily to one side of his head. His features were strong, yet warm and kind, and a carefully trimmed mustache outlined his sensitive mouth. She knew him at once—it was Adam Ladd.

Rebecca felt a quiver of joy as she rose. She wanted to run and greet him, yet she modestly restrained herself. She gathered her flowing skirts and apron about her lithe figure and stepped her high-buttoned shoes smartly along the quarried flagstone walk toward the gravel drive.

Horse and buggy mounted the grade from the bridge, turned into the half-circle drive before the brick house, and drew up at the end of the walk where Rebecca waited winsomely. "What brings you here, Mr. Aladdin?" she inquired with a merry lilt in her voice.

"Business!" Adam's gray eyes sparkled, and his mouth was drawn into a suppressed grin. "But it's not soap for banquet lamp premiums this time," he chuckled, reminding Rebecca of the time he had become her "Mr. Aladdin" by purchasing the entire stock of soap she and Emma Jane Perkins were selling to help the Simpson family.

Quickly he stepped from the carriage, hitched the horse to an iron ring in a granite post, took her hand between both of his, and as if on impulse, drew it to his lips and kissed her fingertips.

Rebecca was thankful that Aunt Jane Sawyer, who was inside the house, could not see her blush at his gallantry.

"Business, Mr. Aladdin?" she inquired, her black eyes wide with wonder. He turned and slid a thin brown leather briefcase from under the seat of the chaise.

"As a matter of fact, yes—business. And I hope to find you agreeable," he continued mysteriously. Then hesitantly he added, "Can we go inside?"

"Of course! It was thoughtless of me not to have asked you!"

Adam guided Rebecca up the steps by her elbow, courteously opening the heavy oaken door.

"Why, Mr. Ladd," exclaimed Aunt Jane, who had come into the front hall at the sound of his carriage, "this is a pleasant surprise!"

"This is a business trip, I assure you, Miss Sawyer," he chuckled. "Can we sit somewhere? I have letters for you both." He held up his case.

"Well . . . well, whatever kin it be about? But do step into the sittin' room," Aunt Jane said, startled.

Rebecca recognized her mother's scratchy handwriting at once as Adam unbuckled his briefcase and drew forth two envelopes. On one was penciled "Sister Jane," and on the other, "Rebecca Rowena." He then pulled forth a sheaf of papers and began to study them as young woman and middle-aged aunt opened their epistles from Sunnybrook.

Dearest Rebecca,

I had not had time to answer your letter last week when Mr. Ladd came to the house and told me that his railway company, the Boston & Down East, wishes to buy Sunnybrook Farm for a new depot. He has offered us $15,000, and since the mortgage is now less than $1,000, there will be plenty left for me and the children. You will get your share, of course, as provided in your father's will.

I do gladly accept your offer to bring the children to live with you and Jane at the brick house—if Jane is willing. I have asked her permission in my letter to her. Mr. Ladd has graciously offered to hire an ambulance to carry me to the station. He will have a railway company Pullman car meet me there so I won't have to sit up during the journey, except for the stagecoach ride to Riverboro.

God is so good to us these days. I'm getting stronger every day and I shall be able to help you and Jane with the housework in just a few weeks.

Your loving mother,
Aurelia Randall

Rebecca's eyes were filled with tears as she raised her head. Aunt Jane, she thought, looked to be between bliss and shock. "Did . . . did Mother tell you how much, Auntie?"

Jane Sawyer nodded, then dabbed her eyes with a lace-fringed hanky. "After all these years, Aurelia is finally going to have enough!" she said firmly.

"My brother John can go to medical college now," Rebecca added. "And sister Hannah's husband can expand his herd of jerseys so that he can support her decently. Will Melville wants so much to make a success of that small farm!"

"These papers," Adam Ladd put in gravely, "are the sale contract. Your mother, Mark, John, and Hannah all have agreed, and of course the young children are provided for. Mrs. Randall insisted I bring them to you personally for your approval before she will sign off."

Rebecca and Jane read the papers carefully. Jane, who had bought and sold several woodlots with money left her by her father, Deacon Israel Sawyer, assured herself and her niece that it was only a standard land contract.

"Is . . . is our old home going to be torn down?" Rebecca inquired earnestly.

Adam chuckled. "Let me advise you that I am only a director of the Boston and Down East Railway Company. After all, I'm only twenty-seven—I'm not the company president yet! Of course, it is entirely possible that the other directors may overrule me. But present plans are to renovate the farmhouse for quarters for the stationmaster and his family. The barn and other outbuildings will be torn down, of course. The tracks will run along the brook, with a trestle by the present cattle ford. We will build a passenger station on the property, near where the Temperance crossroad joins the highway from Portland to Lewiston. Ours is a regular, standard-gauge railway, not just a narrow-gauge jitney, like the present line from Temperance to Maplewood," he said with enthusiasm. "We are tied into lines going to all the major cities in America.

"I think Sunnybrook Station will be a real asset to the community of Temperance," Adam added. "Since there will be a platform for loading milk cans and other market produce, all the farms for miles around will benefit. Our railroad is building a new creamery in Portland, and we shall ship fresh, bottled milk daily from this plant into Boston for delivery before dawn."

Rebecca was so filled with joy that she could hardly speak. Tears welled in her eyes as she said, "So much has happened to me—to my family—this week since Aunt Miranda died. It seems too much all at once. Did Mother tell you the brick house is mine, dear Mr. Aladdin?"

"Why no, no! I knew of course she wished to move in with her sister, here. But I assumed that Miss Jane had invited her herself." Turning to Jane he added with concern, "I don't wish to intrude on your affairs, but where does this leave you? Provided for, I hope, Miss Sawyer?"

"My circumstances have not changed. It's just that I have a new landlady," she said with a prim smile. "When our father, Deacon Israel Sawyer, passed away, he left Miranda the brick house, the outbuildings, the quarter-section farm—160 acres. I got the woodlots, nearly 500 acres. I'm cash poor, but I manage my household expenses nicely enough by selling timber to the sawmill. Now that Rebecca is the new mistress of the brick house, the property continues in the Sawyer family unaltered."

2

FROM THE SACO TO THE ATLANTIC

I should say that having the brick house full of children will change your life-style somewhat," Adam laughed, addressing Aunt Jane.

"After seven years of Rebecca?" Miss Sawyer's voice rose to a querulous pitch as if she were trying to suppress a merry secret. Then in a serious note she added, "Of course, she's grown from the Topsy she was when she first came here to a very accomplished young lady. My sister Miranda once said that proper upbringing and education 'would be the making of Rebecca,' though I surely believe that the Randall in her has contributed more'n some folks would care to credit. God made Rebecca both Randall an' Sawyer in a most happy mix, I think. So I'm ready to see how her brothers and sisters turn out."

Adam smiled, then he checked his watch and reached for his hat and briefcase. "I must be going. My Aunt Mary in North Riverboro is expecting me for supper. It's a three-mile drive with the horse, yet."

"We'd be more'n happy for you to eat with us," Jane politely responded.

"Yes, do—please." Rebecca realized that her heart had spoken. Though Adam was an old and dear friend, he had shown little interest in her beyond the restrained generosity which Rebecca believed grew partially out of a shared sympathy with their similar, wretched early childhood experiences: he an orphan reared by an unmarried aunt; she, having lost her father, had been sent to live with maiden aunts to board and educate. Yet deep within her, Rebecca felt their kinship had to be deeper than mere friendship.

"I'd like to stay—really I would," he responded. "But it's nearly four o'clock. My aunt will be starting to prepare supper any minute now."

"You may use our phone," Jane said, obviously pleased at the chance to offer a guest the opportunity to try out the glistening, proudly waxed oak box with its polished, nickel-plated bells and hard-rubber receiver mounted on the wall in the hall. "When the Saco River Telephone Company ran its lines through Riverboro this summer, I let them install a phone here. With Miranda sick abed, I felt certain it'd be the best way to get the doctor if she needed him in a hurry."

"Did Aunt Miranda approve?" Rebecca's eyes sparkled with glee as she asked.

"Never told her about the phone," Jane tersely replied. "Costs a dollar a month. You kin call your aunt an' get some good out of my expense, Mr. Ladd," she added. "I s'pose you use telephones every day in Boston?"

"Yes, we do. We have gas lights and electric trolley cars, too. Boston is quite a modern city," he modestly remarked. "Where is your phone book?"

"Phone book?" Jane Sawyer was clearly puzzled.

"In Boston they have so many phone customers they publish their names in a phone book, sort of like a dictionary," patiently explained Rebecca, who had heard of such things from friends at Wareham Academy.

"Well, of all things," Jane interjected. "I don't believe I'd want my name and phone number published in a book for everybody to read. You never kin tell who might decide to call. But jest crank up Central—that's Sarah Cobb; she gets paid five dollars a week and her phone free for havin' the switchboard right in her parlor—and give her your aunt's name. She'll call her for you soon's there ain't nobody else usin' the party line in North Riverboro.

"Rebecca, if you kin get me a couple o' pieces o' that split oak from the woodshed to get the kitchen range hot, you can entertain Mr. Ladd while I get supper," Aunt Jane remarked as soon as Adam had made his phone call.

"Oh, Auntie," protested Rebecca, "I shouldn't leave you in the kitchen alone."

"You'll get domesticated soon enough, Rebecca," chuckled Adam. "Come on—I'll help with the firewood."

Once in the woodshed, Rebecca discovered that all the split oak had been used earlier for their breakfast fire. Adam quickly hoisted a large chunk of unsplit oak onto the chopping block as Rebecca grabbed the ax.

He stood back. Rebecca swung. "Thock!" The ax stuck firmly in the center of the chunk of oak.

"Where did you learn to split wood?"

"I haven't," Rebecca admitted. "That's not one of my many talents," she chuckled. "John or Mark always splits it at Sunnybrook. Here Aunt Jane hires Abijah Flagg or a neighbor boy to split and stack the pile. I *can* pluck a chicken though," she added defensively.

Adam twisted the ax from the wood on the block. "It's been a few years since I've had an ax in my hands," he confessed, "but I don't think I've forgotten how." He brought it down easily, flicking the blade deftly as it entered the wood. A stovewood-size piece popped off and shot across the woodshed. "Whack!" Another large chunk split off. Half a dozen easy swings more and the bolt was entirely reduced to manageable splinters.

Rebecca had been gathering an armload as Adam split it. Quickly she disappeared into the kitchen adjacent to the shed. By the time she returned after shaking down the ashes and stoking the firebox of the cast-iron Glenwood range so Aunt Jane could bake a blueberry pie, Adam had littered the shed with the remnants of six more large chunks of oak.

Quickly helping Adam stack the fruit of his labors beside the chopping block, Rebecca protested that they hadn't planned on hiring him as a chore boy. "After all," she said, "only today Aunt Jane said it was time we hired a boy to split and stack this wood for winter. We weren't expecting a railway executive to do our chores, Mr. Aladdin!"

"You may call me 'Adam,'" he protested mildly.

"Mr. Aladdin . . . Adam," Rebecca responded, embarrassed, "could . . . could I show you around? Do you remember the time you found me in my secret chamber in the barn gable?"

"I do indeed! And by all means, show me through your newly acquired estate. These old Maine homesteads have an interesting irregularity not found in city offices and tenements."

Rebecca led the way through the shed in the long ell connecting the house to the barn, which stood some sixty feet to the rear. They passed through the horse stable between, empty now except for a sleigh and a buggy, resting and rusting beneath old tablecloths.

"This is all mine," Rebecca murmured in awe, rolling back the great door leading from the stable in the ell into the cavernous barn, home now only to a side room full of chickens, the doves in the cupola on the roof, an owl, a bat or two, and the wheeling swallows which glided through a missing pane in a window high in the barn's front gable to nurture their young in the wattle-and-daub nests lining the roof between the rafters far above.

Around an old, high-wheeled hayrack, past an idle plow, stepping across a stout, heavy-runnered pung which once had toted Deacon Sawyer's firewood from the forest, and squeezing by a mowing machine half-buried in moldy hay harvested before Rebecca's birth, she led the way straight to the rear of the grand old barn. Its majestic, ten-by-fourteen-inch hand-hewn hemlock beams were as straight and solid as when they had been raised into place more than a hundred years before by Yankee pioneers intent on clearing the wilderness newly won from King George's Redcoats, taking their mustering-out pay in Maine river valley meadowlands and rock-ribbed hills sloping upward toward the White Mountains to the west. Here Abraham Sawyer, Rebecca's grandsire five generations removed, had pulled his stumps with Durham oxen and raised this barn and a cabin and had hung his brown Bess flintlock with its bayonet over his fireplace to take up his plow and scythe. Here, too, his son, Ezekiel Sawyer, had built the sturdy house of bricks burnt in his own kiln of clay mined from the banks of the Saco bordering the Sawyer claims.

At the rear, now, underneath the haymows, Rebecca directed Adam to an old, yet stout ladder leading high up to a loft.

"What's this?" he inquired.

"The old granary is upstairs in the far gable," she explained. "Grandfather Sawyer put his feed grain in with a horse-powered winch through doors up above. Then it would slide down wooden tubes to the cow tie-ups and pig sty. It saved him a lot of work, too!"

"Seems I remember finding you by those doors one fine fall day a few years ago," Adam replied pleasantly. "But I had no idea what was inside." He followed as she climbed the ladder, pushed open a trapdoor, and let herself into a light-filled, empty room above.

They popped into a plank-walled chamber, perhaps ten by fourteen feet square, with two, small, barred doors leading outside. The afternoon October sun slanted through a window in the gable above the doors, too high to see out, but nonetheless flooding the room with light.

"This is my chamber of memories," Rebecca explained solemnly. "But I haven't been up here since I was a student at Wareham Academy. Can it still be here?"

Adam wondered and watched, enraptured, as she climbed upon a bale of straw in a corner, where a comfortable seat, now deep in dust, had been arranged from old feed sacks. Behind the angled brace of a beam she reached blindly and instantly withdrew a little bound book. "Here it is!" she cried with delight, dusting it off. And, flipping through its pages, she quickly spied the spot she was seeking, an entry near the end of the diary.

Dear Diary,

Today Mr. Aladdin came 'round behind the barn seeking me. How I wish he'd come by more often. But my chariots are all pumpkins, I'm afraid.

Rebecca blushed as she realized that Adam was reading it, too. With a snap she closed the book and dropped it into her apron pocket, pulling her sweater over it securely. "There, it's safe," she said with a smile.

Silently Adam turned to the double doors. Unbarring them, he drew the bolt on one, then pushed it open until it stopped against its harness-leather strap which prevented its swinging out of reach. "Last time I saw this door open," he mused, "I was down there under the tree, looking in." He pointed to an old apple tree which had by now dropped its fall fruit and most of its leaves. "And you were up here scribbling nonsense in your silly little book."

"The nonsense of my heart," she replied. Catching his sleeve, Rebecca joined Adam at the open door. With her free hand she pointed to a double row of elms and willows meandering in a graceful curve in the distance beyond the patchwork of haylands, pasture, and the stubble of harvested cornfields. "The Saco River, between those trees," she explained, "is the eastern boundary of the Sawyer farm. Someday I'm going to walk that boundary, then follow the woods and fields back to the road below the village. Meanwhile, we rent the fields out to a neighbor. Do you suppose I'm hoping too much to wish to make this a farm once again? I'm a dreamer, aren't I?"

"Dreams are the stuff of life," he replied firmly. "When I was a boy in North Riverboro, growing up with Aunt Mary, we took the old narrow-gauge train one day from Maplewood to Portland. From that day on I had a dream, a dream of helping the poor village and country folk of Maine with good railways to take their produce to market. If our dreams are dreams of helping others, I believe God will honor those dreams."

"Others have done so much to help me," said Rebecca in reflection. "Aunt Jane and Aunt Miranda put me through Wareham—and now this farm—I want to use it to help others. Do you think that's possible?"

Adam touched her gently on the shoulder. "Very, very possible," he said. "But the salmon that swim up the Saco against the current each spring to leap the rushing falls and spawn in the pleasant, quiet pools must first find their strength while swimming for a time in the broad, wide Atlantic."

3

ABIJAH THE BRAVE AND THE FAIR EMMA JANE

Aunt Jane," said Rebecca the day after Adam Ladd had called at the brick house with the startling news that his railway company was buying Sunnybrook from Aurelia, "Mother will be needing me on the farm to help her pack and to arrange an auction, though I imagine Will Melville will want to buy as much of our livestock as he can afford. I do wish I could bring the cows here and keep them in Grandfather Sawyer's old barn," she added wistfully.

"You'd best be packing then, dear," answered Jane. "Aurelia has had to depend on neighbors to help her for nearly two weeks now. If you miss tomorrow's train from Maplewood, it'll be next week before you can go."

"I'll pack this afternoon. Won't it be grand to have a daily train into Temperance, instead of that old, twice-a-week jitney on the siding from Maplewood," she said happily. "Adam said that the new trunk line through Sunnybrook Farm would take about a year to finish. I surely wish it were done already."

That afternoon, as she had done each day since returning to the brick house, Rebecca seated herself on the front steps for a few moments' relaxation before helping Aunt Jane prepare their evening meal. Her memory ran on Emma Jane Perkins, her dearest friend in Riverboro and former roommate at the Wareham Academy.

Across the river by the bridge, the Perkins's white clapboard cottage stood facing the brick house. Rebecca could see by the black coal smoke billowing from the blacksmith shop behind that Mr. Perkins, "the rich blacksmith," was toiling still at his labors. Since moving his family into Riverboro Village shortly before Rebecca had come there herself, his reputation for quality craftsmanship had made him one of the most successful and prosperous men of the Saco Valley. From sunup 'til sundown, farmers with horses to be shod, mill owners with shafts to be straightened, loggers with chains to be welded brought their problems—and their silver—to his door.

"There comes Emma Jane through her front gate," exclaimed Rebecca, opening her eyes from a brief nod in the afternoon sun. "She will be over here in a minute, and I'll tease her!" Rebecca ran inside and scooted into the sitting room. Pushing up a window sash, she seated herself at the old piano next to the open window.

Peeping from behind the muslin curtains, she waited until Emma Jane was on the very threshold and then began singing her version of an old ballad which she had practiced that morning while she was dressing. Her high, clear voice, quivering with merriment, floated through the windows into the clear autumn air:

A warrior so bold and a maiden so bright
Conversed as they sat on the green.
They gazed at each other in tender delight;

Abijah the Brave was the name of the knight,
And the maid was the Fair Emma Jane.

"Rebecca Randall, stop! Somebody'll hear you!" Emma was now racing through the hall.

"No, they won't—Aunt Jane's making apple jelly in the kitchen, miles away."

"Alas!" said the youth, "since tomorrow I go
To fight in a far distant land,
Your tears for my absence soon ceasing to flow,
Some other will court you, and you will bestow
On the wealthier suitor your hand."

"Rebecca, you can't *think* how your voice carries! I believe Mother can hear it clear over to my house!"

"Then if she can I must sing the third verse, just to clear your reputation from the cloud cast upon it in the second," laughed Emma's tormentor, going on with the song:

"Oh, hush these suspicions!" Fair Emma Jane said,
"So hurtful to love and to me!
For if you be living or if you be dead,
I swear, my Abijah, that none in your stead,
Shall the husband of Emma Jane be!"

After the third verse Rebecca wheeled around on the piano stool and confronted her friend, who was hurriedly closing the sitting room window. "Emma Jane Perkins, it is an ordinary Thursday afternoon at four o'clock, and you have on your new blue dress, although there is not even a church sociable in prospect this evening. Whatever does this mean? Is Abijah the Brave coming back to Riverboro at last?"

"I don't know for certain, but it will be sometime this week."

"And of course you'd rather be dressed up and not seen, than seen when not dressed up. Right, my Fair Emma Jane? So would I! Not that it makes any difference to poor me, wearing my fourth-best black-and-white calico and expecting nobody."

"Oh well, you! There's something inside of you that does instead of pretty dresses," cried Emma Jane, whose adoration of her friend had never altered nor lessened since they met at the age of eleven. "You know you are as different from anybody else in Riverboro as a princess in a fairy story. Libby Moses says they would notice you in Boston!"

"Would they? I wonder," speculated Rebecca, rendered almost speechless by this tribute to her charms. "Well, if Boston could see me, or if you could see me in my lavender muslin dress with the velvet sash, it would die of envy, and so would you," she teased.

"If I had been going to be envious of you, Rebecca, I should have died years ago. Come on—let's go back out on the steps where we can see the fall colors."

"And where we can see the Perkins front gate and the road running both ways," pestered Rebecca. Then softening her tone, she said, "How is it getting on, Emmy? Tell me what's happened at Bowdoin College."

"Nothing much," confessed Emma Jane. "He writes to me, but I don't dare write to him, you know. I don't dare to, 'til he comes to the house."

"Are his letters still in Latin?" asked Rebecca, with a twinkling eye.

"Oh, no! Not now because—well, because there are things you can't seem to write in Latin." Emma Jane was not about to admit that had Abijah written his letters in Latin, she'd have had to ask Rebecca or the minister's wife to translate them.

"You have seen him recently?"

"I saw him at the Sunday school picnic in August, but he won't say anything real to me 'til he dares speak to Mother and Father. He is brave in all other ways, but I'm not sure he'll ever have the courage for that. He's so afraid of them and he always has been. Just remember what's in his mind all the time, Rebecca—that my folks know all about his unmarried mother, and how he was rescued from the county poor farm after she died there. Not that I care. Look how he's gotten educated and worked himself up! I think he's perfectly elergant, and I shouldn't mind if he had been born in the bulrushes, like Moses."

"Moses wasn't born in the bulrushes, Emmy dear," corrected Rebecca with a laugh. "Pharaoh's daughter found him there. It wasn't quite as romantic a scene—Squire Bean's wife taking little Abijah Flagg from the poorhouse after his mother died. But oh, I think Abijah's splendid. Adam Ladd says Riverboro'll be proud of him yet, and I shouldn't wonder, Emmy dear, if you had a three-story house with a cupola on it some day. And sitting down at your mahogany desk inlaid with ivory you will write notes stating that Mrs. Abijah Flagg requests the pleasure of Miss Rebecca Randall's company to tea, and that the Honorable Congressman Flagg will call for her on his way from the station with a fine span of horses."

Emma Jane laughed at the ridiculous prophecy and answered, "If I ever write the invitation I shan't be addressing it to Miss Randall; I'm sure of that. It'll be to Mrs . . ."

"Don't say any morc!" cried Rebecca impetuously, changing color and putting her hand over Emma's lips. "If you won't, I'll stop teasing you. Emmy, dear, I wouldn't tease you either if it weren't something we've both known ever so long—something that you have always consulted me about of your own accord—and Abijah has consulted me, too."

"Don't get excited," replied Emma Jane. "I was only going to say you were sure to be married sooner or later."

"Oh," said Rebecca with a relieved sigh, "if that's all you meant—just nonsense. But I thought, I thought—I don't really know just what I thought you were going to say!"

"I think you thought something you didn't want me to think you thought," said Emma Jane with a knowing smile.

"No, it's not that. But somehow today I have been remembering things. Perhaps it was because at breakfast Aunt Jane reminded me again that I am now the mistress of the brick house, and it will be my task next spring to deal with the farmers who rent the fields. That made me feel very old and responsible. And when I came out on the steps this afternoon, it was just as if pictures of the old years were moving up and down the road. Doesn't the sky look as if it had been dyed blue and the fields painted green and the goldenrod gilded with spun gold this very minute?"

"It's a perfectly elergant day!" responded Emma Jane with a sigh. "If only my mind were at rest. That's the difference between being young and being grown up. We never used to think and worry."

"Indeed we didn't! Look, Emmy, there's the very spot where Uncle Jerry Cobb stopped the stagecoach and I stepped out with my pink parasol and bouquet of purple lilacs into a whole new world for me. And you were watching me from your bedroom window and wondering what I had in Mother's little leather trunk strapped on behind. Poor Aunt Miranda didn't love me at first sight, and oh, how cross she was the first two years! But now every hard thought I ever had about her comes back to me and cuts like a knife!"

"She was dreadfully hard to get along with, and I used to hate her like poison," confessed Emma Jane. "But I am sorry now. She was kinder toward the last anyway, but then you see, children know so little. We never suspected she was sick or that she was worrying over that lost interest money."

"That's the trouble," answered Rebecca. "People seem hard and unreasonable and unjust, and we can't help being hurt at the time. But if they die we forget everything but our own angry speeches. Somehow we never remember theirs. And oh, Emma Jane, there's another sweet little picture out there in the road. The next day after I came to Riverboro, do you remember, I stole out of the brick house crying and leaned against the front gate. You pushed your little, round pink-and-white face through the pickets and said, 'Don't cry! I'll kiss you if you will me!'"

A lump rose suddenly in Emma Jane's throat, and she put her arm around Rebecca's waist as they sat side by side.

"Oh, I do remember," Emma Jane said in a choking voice. "And I can also see the two of us driving over to North Riverboro and selling soap to Mr. Adam Ladd, and lighting up the premium banquet lamp at the Simpson party, and laying the daisies round Jack-o'-Lantern Winslow's mother when she was dead in the cabin, and trundling Jack-o'-Lantern up and down the street in our old baby carriage. And I remember you getting the flag back from Mr. Simpson, and how you looked when you spoke your verses at the flag-raising."

"And have you forgotten," put in Rebecca, "the week I refused to speak to Abijah Flagg because he fished my turban with the porcupine quills out of the river when I hoped that I had lost it at last! Oh, Emma Jane, we had dear, good times together then!"

"I always thought that was an elergant composition of yours—that farewell to the Wareham Academy senior class," said Emma Jane.

"The strong tide bears us on, out of the little harbor of childhood into the unknown seas," recalled Rebecca. "It is bearing you almost out of my sight, Emmy, these last days, when you put on a new dress in the afternoon and look out of the window instead of coming across the bridge. Abijah Flagg never used to be in the little harbor with the rest of us. When did he first sail in, Emmy?"

4

THE LITTLE HARBOR

Emma Jane Perkins grew a deeper pink, and her buttonhole of a mouth quivered with delicious excitement as she considered how to answer Rebecca's query. "It was at the academy when he wrote me his first Latin letter from Bowdoin College in Brunswick," she said in a half-whisper. "I realized then how much I really cared for Abijah Flagg."

"I remember that letter," laughed Rebecca. "Suddenly the Latin dictionary took the place of the crochet needle in your affections. It was cruel of you never to show me that letter, Emmy!"

"I know every word of it by heart," said the blushing Emma Jane, "and I think I really ought to say it to you, because it's the only way you will ever know how perfectly elergant Abijah is. Shall I have to translate it for you, because it seems to me I could not bear to do that!"

"It depends upon Abijah's Latin and your pronunciation," teased Rebecca.

The Fair Emma Jane, looking none too old still for the "little harbor," but almost too young for the "unknown seas," gathered up her courage and recited tremulously the boyish love letter that had so fired her youthful imagination.

"Vale carissima, carissima puella!" repeated Rebecca in her musical voice, "'Farewell dearest, dearest maiden.' Oh, how beautiful it sounds! I don't wonder it altered your feelings for Abijah. Upon my word, Emma Jane," she cried with a sudden change of tone, "if I had suspected for an instant that Abijah the Brave had that Latin letter in him, I should have tried to get him to write it to me. And then it would be I who would sit down at my mahogany desk and ask Miss Perkins to come to tea with Mrs. Flagg."

Emma Jane paled and shuddered openly. "I speak as a Christian sister, Rebecca," she said, "when I tell you I've always thanked the Lord that you never looked at Abijah Flagg and he never looked at you. If either of you ever had, there never would have been a chance for me, and I've always known it!"

At this, Rebecca laughed in spite of herself. "Emmy, dear, you *must* know I was teasing again. Abijah has been like a brother to me—the older brother I never had. When I would spend hours with him, teaching him to read, helping him with his geometry and Latin until he could pass the entrance exams at Bowdoin, we surely had ample time for romance, were there to have been any! I'm sure he has thought of me as a sister only."

Abijah Flagg, though an orphan of uncertain origins, was a true child of his native state. Something of the same timber that Maine puts into her forests, something of the same strength and resisting power that she works into her rocks goes into her sons and daughters. And at twenty-two, Abijah was going to take his fate in his hands and ask Mr. Perkins, the well-to-do blacksmith, if after a suitable period of probation, during which he would complete his education, he might marry the Fair Emma Jane.

This was young love, perhaps, but even that may develop into something larger, truer, and finer. And not so far away from Rebecca were other and different hearts growing and budding, each in its own way. There was Miss Dearborn, the pretty schoolteacher, drifting into a foolish alliance because she did not agree with her stepmother at home. There was Herbert Dunn, valedictorian of his class, dazzled by Huldah Meserve, who like a firefly shone bright at a distance, but close at hand, had neither heat nor light. There was sweet Emily Maxwell of Wareham, less than thirty, still, with most of her heart bestowed on her students. She was toiling on at Wareham Academy, living as unselfish a life as a nun in a convent, pouring out her mind, soul, heart, and body on her chosen work. How many women give themselves thus, consciously and unconsciously! And though they themselves miss the joys and compensations of mothering their own little twos and threes, God must be grateful to them for their mothering of hundreds.

Then there was Adam Ladd, waiting for a certain girl to grow a little older, simply because he could not find one already grown to suit his somewhat fastidious and exacting tastes.

"I'll not call Rebecca perfection," he stated once in a letter to Miss Maxwell. "I'll not call her perfection, for that's a post afraid to move. But she's the dancing sprig of the tree next to it."

When first Rebecca appeared on his aunt's porch in North Riverboro and insisted on selling him a large quantity of soap in order that her friends, the Simpsons, might possess a premium in the form of a greatly needed banquet lamp, she had riveted his attention. He thought at the time that he enjoyed talking with her more than with any girl or woman alive, and he had never changed his opinion. She always caught what he said as if it were a ball tossed to her. As his thoughts passed through her mind, they came back to him dyed with deeper colors.

In his heart Adam Ladd always called Rebecca his "Little Spring." His boyhood had been lonely and unhappy; that part of life he had missed. And although he was now enjoying the full summer of success and prosperity, he found his lost youth only in her.

Do you remember an early day in May with budding leaf, warm earth, tremulous air, and changing, willful sky—how new it seemed? How fresh and joyous beyond all explaining?

Have you lain with half-closed eyes where the flickering of sunlight through young leaves, the song of birds and brook, and the fragrance of wildflowers combined to charm your senses, and you felt the sweetness and grace of nature as never before?

Rebecca was springtime to Adam's thirsty heart. She was blithe youth incarnate; she was music—an Aeolian harp that every passing breeze woke to some whispering little tune. She was a changing, iridescent bubble of joy; she was the shadow of a leaf dancing across the dusty floor of his soul. No bough of his thought could be so bare, but she somehow built a nest in it and evoked life where none was before.

And Rebecca herself?

She had been quite unconscious of all this until very lately, and even now she was but half-awakened, sorting out her childish instincts and her girlish dreams, seeking the Lord daily for His direction, His deliverance from her own willful impulses, searching for the light that would guide her safely through the labyrinth of her new sensations.

For the moment she was absorbed, or thought she was, in the little love story of Abijah and Emma Jane, but in reality, had she realized it, that love story served chiefly as a basis of comparison for a possible one of her own.

Emma Jane had gone home, and Rebecca had eaten supper with Aunt Jane. Afterward Rebecca placed her suitcase—the small leather trunk her mother had lent her seven years earlier—just inside the front door to be ready for her coach ride to the Maplewood depot in the morning. The early fall evening was fast drawing upon the brick house, and she drew Aunt Miranda's wool sweater about her shoulders and seated herself on the doorstep for one last meditation before departing for Sunnybrook.

A blue dress caught Rebecca's eye at one of the Perkins's windows and showed that in one heart hope was not dead yet, although it was nearly six o'clock. Suddenly there was the sound of a horse's feet coming up the quiet street. A little open vehicle came in sight, and in it sat Abijah Flagg. The rented livery stable buggy was so freshly painted and so shiny in the rays of the setting sun that Rebecca thought he must have alighted just outside the village and given it a last polish. The creases of his trousers, too, had an air of having been pressed only a few minutes before. The buggy whip was new, and it had a yellow ribbon on it; his suit was new, and the coat flourished a flower in its buttonhole. The hat, a snappy silk bowler derby, was the latest thing, and the determined swain wore a seal ring on the little finger of his right hand, which caught a glint of the last rays of the setting sun. As Rebecca remembered the many times she had guided this hand in making capital letters in his copybook, she felt positively maternal, although she was much younger than Abijah the Brave.

He drove up to the Perkins's gate and was so long about hitching the horse that Rebecca's heart beat tumultuously at the thought of Emma Jane waiting inside. He brushed an imaginary speck off his sleeve, drew on a pair of kid gloves, went up the path, rapped at the knocker, and went in.

Not all heroes go to the wars, thought Rebecca. *Abijah has laid the ghost of his wild father to rest and redeemed the memory of his forsaken mother, for no one will dare say again that he will never amount to anything!*

The minutes went by, and more minutes, and more. The tranquil dusk settled down over the little village street, and the orange October moon hung just behind the top of the Perkins's majestic pine next to the blacksmith shop.

The Perkins's front door opened, and Abijah the Brave came out hand in hand with his Fair Emma Jane.

They walked through the orchard, the full moon lighting their way beneath the bare apple limbs, the eyes of Emma's parents following them from the window, and just as they disappeared down the shadowy slope that led to the riverside, the dark coat sleeve encircled the blue serge waist.

Rebecca, quivering with instant empathy and comprehension, hid her face in her hands. *Emmy has sailed away, and I am all alone in the little harbor,* she thought.

It was as if childhood, like a thing real and visible, were slipping down the grassy riverbank after Abijah and Emma Jane, and disappearing like them into the moonlit shadows of the autumn evening.

"I am all alone in the little harbor," she repeated. "And oh, I wonder, I wonder, shall I be afraid to leave it if anybody ever comes to carry me out to sea!"

They walked through the orchard,
the full moon lighting their way.

5

SETTLING AFFAIRS AT SUNNYBROOK

Sunnybrook Farm was in its yearly glory of dying autumn splendor. Rebecca's eyes moistened as she rode up the farm's long drive from the crossroad with Will Melville, her sister Hannah's husband. She surveyed the broad acres outlined with elms, yellow now with autumn leaves, which marched down their little valley along the ragged, tumbledown stone walls dividing the fields. The brook she spied beyond the willows and alders, silent now from its choir of summer frogs. Past the ramshackle old barn they drove—though wanting in shingles and windowpanes, it still bustled with the bleat of calves and the brown grunts of pigs. The Cape Cod cottage came next into view, sturdy still, but in need of new gutters and paint.

This lonely hollow was the land of her nativity. Now it had been sold, and soon her family must move.

Back to the brick house in Riverboro they would go, where her mother had grown up and Rebecca herself had spent her teen years. But dear old Sunnybrook—how her heart ached when she realized it would be hers to cherish but a few weeks longer. Yet Rebecca was no longer a child. "You can't go home again," Miss Maxwell, her mentor at Wareham, had warned her more than once, she recalled.

Pictures swam in her mind, pictures of her father, Lorenzo Randall, playing his old violin, the bow gliding across the strings lighter than a fairy slipper as it emitted sweeter melodies than even a Stradivarius could have produced, she was sure. The strains of Russian, Polish, and German composers in turn mingled each evening with the steam of her mother's cooking and the murmur of childish voices beneath the low-beamed ceiling of the great room of their old cottage. Only occasionally did Lorenzo Randall lapse into "Turkey in the Straw" or "Arkansas Traveler." Such tunes, he was wont to explain, cheapened a fine instrument and too often left tiny ears tinny and insensitive to higher musical tastes. Tears of reminiscent joy rolled down Rebecca's cheeks as she recalled her father's rendition of "Danny Boy," and her mother's beautiful contraltro voice as she sang softly to his tune.

Somewhere under the attic rafters, Rebecca knew, that old musical instrument lay in its dust-laden leather case. She recalled that her mother had once tried to sell it when a mortgage deadline pressed. "One dollar," the shopkeeper in Lewiston had scornfully remarked. "That's my best offer for an old fiddle of uncertain origin." Aurelia had spent two dollars for a round-trip train ticket to Lewiston from Temperance; and since Temperance siding's trains ran only twice weekly, she would need to put up two nights with friends in the city. But, "It's worth a hundred, at least. My husband wouldn't have owned a cheap instrument," she had stoutly defended its value, returning it to its case as she left the pawn shop.

Sunnybrook Farm

Will's "Hup! Ho! Whoa, girl!" to his mare brought Rebecca back to the present as he drew the carriage between the well sweep and the sweet apple tree to stop at the cottage's front door stoop. Rebecca entered and was amazed to see her mother seated in a cane-backed, wooden wheelchair, a gingham apron draped over her legs, as she mended a pair of John's pants across her knees.

"Mother," she exclaimed, "surely you're not supposed to be out of bed!"

"This is my third day up, Rebecca. I sat up for two hours this morning, and I've been up nearly three this afternoon. There's work to be done," she teased, holding up the pair of britches.

Next day, Saturday, Rebecca, brothers John and Mark, Hannah, and Will Melville sat with Aurelia for a family council. "Mr. Ladd was here yesterday, and he has promised to come by Tuesday with the settlement papers, a check for fifteen thousand dollars, and also to bring Vice President Hobson from the branch bank. Mr. Hobson will bring the old mortgage, and Mr. Ladd says Hobson can set us up with bank accounts without even leaving the house. But oh, Rebecca, what if he changes his mind? What if the railway directors won't pay what he's promised?"

Aurelia Randall's pessimism had grown out of years of false hopes from Lorenzo's many attempts at investing the money she had inherited from her father, Deacon Israel Sawyer. Sunnybrook was the one security that had not slipped beyond their grasp before they could pluck its fruit. Was this to melt away also?

"Mother," Rebecca put in firmly, "I read that contract myself. It was *already* signed by the Boston and Down East's directors. Aunt Jane says all it needs is your signature, witnessed and notarized. All that remains is for us to get paid." She grinned impishly as she fished out a long manila envelope which she had been hiding between the folds of a *Portland Press-Herald* on her lap. Barely containing her glee, Rebecca withdrew with trembling fingers a sheaf of legal-sized papers and unfolded them in triumph. "Mr. Ladd left this in my care," she said, slipping into gravity at the awesomeness of the occasion. "He said that all these papers need is your notarized signature, Mother," she repeated. "Sunnybrook will then belong to the railway, and they will owe us fifteen thousand dollars. Just be sure he hands you the check with one hand as you place the contract in his other!" she chuckled.

"Well . . . well, I guess we don't need to worry about that," Aurelia murmured. "And the papers do say we have three months to move, don't they, Rebecca?"

"They surely do, Mother," Rebecca piped. "That gives us the rest of the year, if we need it." Carefully she folded the papers, returned them to their envelope, then ceremoniously pigeonholed them in her mother's old Governor Winthrop desk, which for twenty years had been Sunnybrook's business center with Aurelia as bookkeeper.

"Now," she cried triumphantly, "shall we get on with the business?"

"I nominate Rebecca for business manager for the rest of our stay here," Aurelia said cheerfully. "What do you say, children?"

"Yes, do, Rebecca!" they chorused, almost in unison.

"All right," agreed Rebecca. "As I see it, we've got two matters to take care of: we've got to pack our clothes and what furniture we plan to keep for ourselves to move to Riverboro. And we've got to sell the rest."

"How about an auction?" Will put in, with the assertiveness that Hannah had found so attractive when she had married him. Though Rebecca had already considered an auction, and had even discussed it with her mother, she said nothing, wisely letting Will believe his idea to be original. "Harvest will soon be over," Will continued, "and farmers from miles around will turn out for all-day auctions all across the country. 'Course I'd like first chance at a couple of the best heifers and some of the farm equipment," he added sheepishly.

"Like Father's old horse rake you 'borrowed' three summers ago," commented Hannah, his wife, with mock indignation.

"I *do* lend it back when John has need of it to rake the back fields," he protested. "Anyway, if my machinery shed hadn't kept it dry, the wood-spoke wheels would've rotted off by now!"

"Will, I delegate you to appraise the cattle," Rebecca directed. "And John, can you compare prices on used farm machinery at the Trading Post in Temperance? And since I shall be driving over to Lewiston Monday to talk with auctioneer Ralph 'Razor' Richardson, I'll also look in at a couple of secondhand furniture stores for ideas on what our extra bedsteads and chests of drawers are worth—that is, if Will will let me use his driving horse and buggy."

"No problem, Becky," Will replied. "But are you sure you can deal with a big-city auctioneer?" he asked merrily.

❧ ❧ ❧

Monday evening a very discouraged Rebecca drove Will's rig into Sunnybrook's yard just at dusk. She left the horse and wagon with Mark to return to Will, then went straight to where John was milking the last of their four jerseys. "John," she cried, "'Razor' Richardson's secretary says he's booked solid until the end of the year. The other two auction houses in Lewiston told me the same thing."

"God will work things out, Becky dear." John smiled bravely as he poured the milk through a cheesecloth strainer into the cream separator in the shed beside the barn.

"That's not all," she added indignantly. "Old bureaus are selling for as little as fifty cents in the city. Five dollars will buy a nice used solid maple highboy—with dovetailed drawers and solid brass handles, and the varnish in near-perfect condition."

"Don't take it so hard," John said pleasantly. "I've been doin' some arithmetic today myself. We've got forty tons of good hay in the mow and thirty bushels of oats, and about as much corn. At two dollars a bushel for the corn and two-fifty for the oats, that's a hundred and thirty dollars, more or less. Add to that at least ten bushels of dry yelloweyed beans in that pile of vines at the end of the barn floor—after Mark gets done thrashin' 'em out with his flail—at five dollars a bushel for the beans, we've got more profit from Sunnybrook than ever before. The cattle will need very little feed until they're sold, since they're still on pasture. We should keep a bushel of beans and a barrel of potatoes to take to the brick house, of course."

"The oats and corn and beans will sell for sure," said Rebecca, her spirits picking up. "But the hay?" she queried. "It's been a good year for hay, you said. Most folks' barns must be full, like ours. What we can sell at the auction—if there *is* any auction—won't pay for pitching it out of the haymow!"

John grinned. "Plenty of hay—and barns *are* full all over the state o' Maine—means we'll get a good price for our cattle, because feed is cheap locally, and farmers will figure they can afford to winter 'em. Will came by here only two hours ago. He hitched a ride over to Arthur Tuttle's cattle brokerage to see what Tut was payin' for cows and calves. Our best milkers are worth at least seventy-five dollars; more, if we can get the bidding goin'. And even a runt calf is worth five.

"But, hey!" John went on, "you were no sooner out of sight this morning when Elmer Barnes' steam hay press, engine and all, came up the road behind his four Belgian horses. I wasn't paying much attention. I mean, I was getting my eyes full of that big, new coal-fired boiler and steam engine, not even thinking about the hay in our barn when he drew his horses up and offered me fifty cents to water them from our well. 'Course I asked him where he was going."

"And?"

"And he said he had three farms lined up between here and Temperance—Hardin's, Dowe's, and Fletcher's—each with twenty or thirty tons of extra hay to press. He figures that'll keep him busy two or three weeks."

"But with everyone else in the hay business, how are we going to sell all that hay? Will there be anything left after we've paid to have it pressed into bales?"

John looked immensely pleased with himself as he answered, "Mr. Barnes said that with the drought in southern New England and New York state this past summer, hay is scarce south of here, and the livery stables in New York City are paying a premium price—ten dollars a ton—I *mean* ten dollars a ton at the freight docks in Maine, actually! And they've sent brokers all over to buy it. So I used Hannah's phone to ring up the depot master in Temperance, and he told me he has been given advertisements by three brokers in the past two weeks. Ten dollars *is* the going price for baled hay, though locally unpressed hay is selling for not more than three. So after paying Barnes two dollars for pressing, that leaves us eight dollars a ton times forty tons of hay—three hundred and twenty dollars," he coolly estimated.

"That's . . . that's a lot of money!"

"You bet. Sunnybrook hasn't paid us over three hundred a year since I can remember."

"But we've got to hire a crew to handle the hay, haven't we? I've heard those big commercial bales weigh two hundred pounds apiece!"

"Barnes has all he can do running his press and stoking the steam engine, that's for sure," John said thoughtfully. "But I figure that Mark and I can work together stacking the bales and helping feed the hay press. I'm sure Will will help for a spell, too. That leaves us needing a couple of guys to pitch down from the mow."

"I haven't forgotten how to use a pitchfork, and if Hannah can help, I'm sure Jenny and Fanny are big enough now to tend her baby and take care of Mother in the house. If Mother were able, she'd be out here pitching herself."

"Mother's climbed her last hayloft ladder, I'm afraid," John said quietly.

Next day, Tuesday, after Aurelia had signed the papers and banker Hobson had notarized them and the checks had been exchanged for bank books, Rebecca explained the dilemma of needing an auctioneer to Adam Ladd.

"Your instincts are quite correct about this being a good time of year for an auction," said Adam. "The auction houses all know that, too — that's why they're booked way ahead. There'll be auctioneers available during the winter after Christmas, but you'd hardly draw a crowd then. Why don't you be your own auctioneer?"

"I . . . I . . . why — that takes a special talent," Rebecca stammered.

"Indeed it does!" Rebecca thought he sounded a bit smug when he said it. "I shall never forget one very talented young saleslady who sold me two entire cases of quite ordinary soap in North Riverboro!" Adam added.

Rebecca brightened. "I can sell, all right, can't I? But doesn't an auctioneer need a license of some kind? Besides, I can't talk like an auctioneer."

"You don't need a license to sell your *own* property," Adam assured her. "And as for the way you talk, what's important is, will people buy? You certainly can *sell!* Keep your wits about you, and appoint someone who's good at figures to keep records and handle the cash."

Aurelia Randall, who had wheeled her chair into the kitchen to check on Jenny and Fanny, who were cooking the noon meal, now returned to the sitting room. "Rebecca could sell mosquito repellent to polar bears," her mother told Adam. "When she was only eight she raised Christmas money by selling wreaths in the village of Temperance two miles away faster than Hannah and I could make 'em. But dinner's ready. Won't you stay? I guess your friend, Mr. Hobson, has left already," she added, peering out the window at his top buggy disappearing down the lane.

Adam was about to decline the offer, but he caught Rebecca's imploring glance and his heart turned to butter. "As a matter of fact, yes," he answered. "I'm driving to Lewiston this evening in my rented rig, but my train for Boston doesn't leave until morning. So I do have a little time yet."

6

THE AUCTION

May I show you what you've bought, Mr. Ladd?" Rebecca queried as soon as they had dined. "Surely your directors in Boston will want a report."

"Actually, they have a pretty good idea what we've bought, and so do I." He opened his briefcase and produced a hand-drawn map, professionally rendered in India ink on heavy paper. "Perhaps you'd like to see what the surveyors were doing on your farm this summer." He spread it out on the kitchen table, now cleared of its dishes by Rebecca's busy sisters. "See here."

Rebecca, Aurelia, and the boys looked at the document, amazed. Every crook of the brook across their little eighty acres was drawn in minute detail. Every knoll, every hummock was given with its elevation. A railroad was shown running straight as an arrow along the streamside, crossing the oxbow bend on a trestle, then recrossing as the brook meandered in the other direction.

Outside, Rebecca took Adam's polite elbow, and the couple strolled toward the back fields, where the railway map had shown the trestle. "I'll get a crick in my shoulder if you continue hanging on to my elbow like a puppy," Adam remarked pleasantly as soon as they had passed a bend in the ruts that passed for a wagon road to the hayfields down by the brook. "I've a better idea," he teased, reaching for her hand. "Let's walk like this, instead."

"Since we're wearing gloves, I'm sure Mother won't mind if we hold hands." Impishly she presented her cotton-gloved hand to his, dressed in calfskin.

"Come on. Enough of this silliness," he answered. Hand in hand they strolled toward the intervale along the brook, the grass at their ankles already tipped with brown by early fall frosts. Around a second bend they came upon a majestic weeping willow growing on a knoll which sloped toward the brookside fields beyond. Rebecca knelt here at once, weeping, and she quickly parted the branches, yellow with fall leaves, as she did so.

"Why, what's the matter?" Adam, compassionate and concerned, was perturbed. Quickly he held the branches back for a better look. Beneath the canopy he spied a child's granite gravestone with this inscription:

Little Mira, how we miss you,
Your gentle voice no more we'll hear;
For you've left and gone to heaven
Where there is no pain nor care.

Miranda Randall
1882–1888

In closer to the tree, so close, in fact, that it was tipped at an angle by the intruding roots, a larger stone said simply:

Lorenzo de Medici Randall
1844–1882

"Your little sister and your father?" Adam inquired, putting his arm about Rebecca's trembling shoulders.

"Yes . . . oh, it's going to be hard to say good-by to them," she sobbed.

"In reality you said good-by to them years ago," Adam gently reminded her.

Composing herself, Rebecca pointed to Lorenzo's gravestone by the tree trunk. "I planted this willow myself. It was only a tree branch when I stuck it next to Father's stone a dozen years ago. I watered it all that first summer, and how it has grown in just a few years!"

"God is the giver of life," responded Adam. "Some life matures rapidly, like this tree; some grows more slowly." He seemed to have more meaning than what he spoke, Rebecca thought, but Adam said no more.

"What . . . what will become of these graves, now that the railroad has bought Sunnybrook?" she asked earnestly. "Will we need to have them moved to the cemetery by the Temperance Meeting House?"

"You could do that, of course. But it seems an unnecessary expense." Adam studied the landscape for a moment, then continued. "The graves are not at all in the way, either of the tracks or of any planned development," he said. "With your permission, I shall have the Boston and Down East Railway Company build a wrought-iron fence encompassing an acre, with this tree in the center—we'll prune the tree, of course. The fence shall have granite posts, and above the gate in iron letters it will say, 'Randall Cemetery.'"

"It should say 'Sunnybrook,'" said Rebecca.

"Sunnybrook Cemetery?"

"Just say 'Sunnybrook,'" Rebecca corrected him firmly.

"My life seems so confused now, Adam," Rebecca remarked after they had passed on to the meadows below. "So many wonderful things have happened. The sale of this farm, which Mother couldn't possibly keep any longer. John free to go to medical college, and money in hand for his books and tuition. But now, instead of a career, I'm responsible for the brick house. I've always felt that God wanted me to teach, or something—to use my life to help others. If I spend it managing the brick house and its farm, as Aunt Miranda did, the money she spent on me will all be wasted, I'm afraid."

"Are you asking me for advice? I've got problems of my own that I can't seem to solve. But just a couple of thoughts, if I may. If you believe the Lord is calling you to pursue a career, then you should seriously consider it. Surely your mother and your Aunt Jane can manage the brick house quite nicely. Your mother's years of experience running Sunnybrook Farm are worth a great deal, I'd say. She'll need a little incentive, of course."

"Such as?"

"A portion of the profits from renting out the fields."

"She can have it all, of course! But Adam, I'm worried that Mother's share of the land sale money will slip through her fingers."

"Let me show you something." Adam withdrew a writing pad from his inside suit pocket, on which he had scribbled some notes. "The sale of the produce and goods from the auction will keep Aurelia and the three younger children for at least a year—maybe two. By then she'll have the first interest check from the bank. The interest alone will pay your mother at least a dollar a day—not wealth, perhaps, but with no mortgage or rent to pay, and the rental from the fields at the brick house paying the taxes for you and some left for her, she will have more than ample to live on."

Rebecca, wise as she was, could not fathom what anyone could do to spend more than a dollar every single day of the year. "Sounds as though you've got it all figured out," she laughed. "But you said you had problems, too? Perhaps I can help."

"Well, yes, the kind of problem that many a man would envy, I'm afraid. But I'm not sure what you can do to help."

"Oh?"

"As I told you last week in Riverboro, from my childhood I dreamed of building a railway that would connect these backcountry farms to the markets on a daily basis. Now that that dream is nearly realized, I can look ahead to more railroads, more profits, more wealth. The rails help the farmers, true. But other men besides me can build them!"

"And other women can manage brick houses," Rebecca added affirmatively.

"Exactly. I feel the need to invest my time, my talents, my life in something more personal, more directly involved with helping others, and I'm not certain that the railroad business will be the best way to do this in future years."

"I see what you mean," Rebecca mused. "But what's this?" Glad for an excuse to change the nettlesome topic, she pointed to a small stake with numbers penciled on it half hidden in the grass.

"That's a grade stake. The surveyors put it there to show the engineers where to start building the trestle. You will find them all along both sides of the brook. The new trestle will cross the stream here, and beyond the oxbow bend it will cross again."

"And it will destroy my froggery!" she moaned.

"Froggery?" Adam was puzzled.

"Hannah and I used to grow frogs in a little pond we built out of cedar rails under the alder bushes in the bog next to the stream," she said with childish animation. "We'd use an old flower pot to fill our pond with frog eggs from along the edge of the brook. Then we'd watch them hatch throughout the spring."

"Sounds exciting," he teased.

"More exciting than you'd think. One June a mean old blue heron waded in and caught every last one of my tadpoles before they got their legs and could hop away!" Rebecca parted the bushes at the edge of the field and began to make her way through the underbrush.

"That's no place for a man in a business suit," Adam protested.

"Oh, come on! We've had a dry October. You'll not get your fancy kangaroo leather shoes wet if you're careful to step on tufts."

Together they wound through the bushes toward the stream. Almost there, Rebecca paused at a large clump of bulrushes, then peered within. "There it is!" she exclaimed. "Just as I remember it." Carefully she trod on dry tufts of swale grass as Adam followed.

Splash!

"Silly muskrat," Rebecca cried, pointing to the ripples on the water just beneath an old log extending across the tiny pond. "He's using our catwalk for a diving board. We dragged that across there, oh, so long ago, so we could sit on it and dip for our tadpoles and pollywogs without getting all wet."

"Sounds like you were quite the engineer."

"Actually, I almost got a whipping for that one," she confessed. "Hannah and I dragged that log from where a beaver was cutting trees in a poplar grove just upstream. When we got it here, we found that to get it into place, one of us would have to wade across. We'd been wading a lot anyway, of course, so I just hiked my skirts up under my belt and went in up to my bloomers. Then I tripped on a root. I got soaked, of course, so I simply sloshed around in the mud while we finished the job."

"What did your mother say?"

"She said she didn't mind my getting myself wet. Actually, she always thought it unfair that boys could go swimming while girls could only wade. Mother never believed that old story about how cold water hurts a woman's constitution."

"But you said you got in trouble?"

"My clothes weren't only wet—they were full of mud, which Mother did not appreciate. She made me do the entire family wash on a scrub board in a wooden tub."

At that, Rebecca stepped up on the log bridge.

"Where are you going?"

"Going? I can still walk on a log. I'm not walking with a cane, yet!"

"Rebecca, poplar logs rot . . ."

Ker-splash! Rebecca sat down suddenly as the log broke in half under her. She found herself sitting on the rotten log, up to her armpits in the icy water.

Adam considered diving in after her, but since there seemed to be no imminent danger, he decided prudence to be the better part of valor. "Shall I come in after you?" he offered, half in jest.

"I think one of us with wet clothes is quite enough," she spluttered. Then bravely smiling, Rebecca said, "You see, I'm still quite a little girl!"

"When I said I felt a need to use my life to help others, pulling wet damsels out of muddy frog ponds wasn't quite what I had in mind!" Adam gave her his hand as she clambered back onto more-or-less dry ground. Though she protested fervently, Adam slipped his black cashmere topcoat over her shoulders, bare now except for a thin, wet cotton dress, since she had peeled off her sodden sweater to wring it out.

"What will Mother say?" Rebecca fumed in disgust at herself.

❧ ❧ ❧

"I guess I'm always needing your help—I'm such a bother," Rebecca later remarked, after she had changed into dry clothes and Adam was drying his coat by the parlor stove just before leaving for Lewiston. "There's one thing I'd appreciate having you stay out of, though."

"What's that?" Adam was puzzled.

"Our auction. Unless I miss my guess, you'd buy anything you didn't think was selling high enough."

He grinned. "What's wrong with that?"

"Whatever happened to trusting the Lord?"

"You're right, I suppose. Tell you what. If you don't forbid me to come to the auction, I promise not to bid on anything unless it's something I want very badly."

"You're a dear!" Rebecca laughed at him impishly.

❧ ❧ ❧

In the weeks that followed, Rebecca again followed her instincts to turn a profit from many seemingly insignificant items around the house and farm. Since Adam Ladd had said, "The barn is going to be torn down, anyway; you might as well strip it of anything of worth," her mercenary eyes alighted first on several dozen loose, dry hardwood timbers of the now-empty hay scaffold. At her request, Mark rolled these down and then dragged them outside with a chain and the horses. John borrowed a buzz saw and a one-lung gasoline engine from a neighbor, and with

Mark's help he quickly turned these logs into several cords of excellent, dry stove wood to sell. Some very fortunate Temperance housewife would bake her biscuits and pies all that winter on coals from rock maple seasoned more than half a century in the Sunnybrook Farm's haymow.

The selling fever had put the entire family into high gear. John's mind brightened one day like the mantel of an overheated Aladdin oil lamp when he decided that, since the family would surely move to Riverboro by Thanksgiving, little winter firewood would be needed. Aurelia was shocked one day in early November to see a dray wagon from the village loading the wood from her shed. Had not Rebecca intervened, she'd have broken her cane over the poor man's head.

Mark, notorious for broken bones, even shinnied to the barn ridge to rescue for the auction the fine copper weathercock which had pointed into the Atlantic breezes for three quarters of a century.

There were so many useful items in the house and barn to sell—china dolls, old cradles, a butter churn, pins, needles, buttons, nails, screws, odds and ends of cloth and thread, half-filled bottles of medicines for man and beast, bolts with nuts and bolts without—too many to sell separately. So Rebecca hit upon the scheme of putting Jenny and Fanny to work packaging and labeling. Small items went into old canning jars. Mark scoured the neighborhood with Will's horse and wagon to procure boxes and crates, and when the supply ran out, he proceeded to nail together another dozen from old barn boards.

Auction day arrived, just a week before Thanksgiving. The old barn had been swept clean, and John and Mark had built a low platform at one end of the barn floor. Aurelia, who had by then graduated from a wheelchair to a rocking chair, sat behind a small table with a cash box. By nine o'clock the yard was filled with buggies, surries, and farm wagons; and the drive was lined with vehicles and horses clear to the highway.

"We're selling the household goods first," Rebecca decided firmly, against her mother's protests. Will Melville, who had come with a pocketful of greenbacks, determined to go home with the two best heifers and a bull calf, agreed. "Once a farmer buys a cow, he'll take his family and go home," Will pointed out to his mother-in-law. "Then there's that many fewer customers. But if he gets his eye on a prize animal, he'll stay until he's had a chance to bid on it."

As the morning passed, no one but Rebecca was surprised that she sold item after item, boxfull after boxfull, at greater than market prices. She'd quote a poem, make up a limerick, or demonstrate the object for sale until the crowd laughed itself into loosening its purse strings.

One item though, her father's old violin, she saved until late afternoon when John and Mark had led the last cow and calf and sheep and goat through the barn, and numbers of farmers had departed, either to take their new-found livestock home or to do their evening chores. Sadly she picked up the instrument and opened the case. Quoting a few lines from "The Touch of the Master's Hand" with as much animation as she could muster, she held it aloft. After a pause, "What am I bid?"

"Two dollars."

"Three!"

"I hear three. Who'll make it five?"

"Five," came the bored response from a farmer chewing a straw on the sidelines.

"Five once. Going. Five twice."

"Wait!" A tall young man in citified clothing, who had come late to the auction and who stood, arms folded, his

He tucked it carefully under his chin and drew the bow lightly.

felt hat drawn over his eyes, just outside the circle of lantern light illuminating the early evening of November, strode to the platform. “Let me see it.”

Rebecca passed it to him at once, as she realized that it was Adam. Instinctively she knew something good was about to happen.

Adam held the old violin to his ear and tightened its four strings, plucking them one by one. He tucked it carefully under his chin and drew the bow lightly. The strains of “Abide with Me” held the audience entranced for several minutes. “The Love of God” then moved several to tears. He passed it back to Rebecca and took a seat on the front row.

“How much am I bid?” Though her voice had hushed to a whisper, she spoke with such clarity that Adam imagined an angel was speaking from the rafters above him.

“Twenty-five!” came at once; then, “Thirty!” “Fifty!” soon followed. Adam himself bid seventy-five.

“Ninety!” from the back row.

“One hundred!” It was Adam, and no one there could, or would, challenge the Boston gentleman’s right to the violin any longer.

“Adam,” Rebecca later exclaimed, “I . . . I didn’t know you could play!”

“My Aunt Mary insisted that I take lessons when I was a kid. And yes, I still play—I give concerts on the corner of the Boston Common by Park Street Church on Sunday afternoons during the summer months each year.”

“But you bid so . . . so much!”

“I need a good violin. I hadn’t planned on buying it, but once I got it in my hands, I knew by its feel I was holding a very fine instrument. In fact, it appears to be a rather good copy of a Stradivarius.”

Sadly Rebecca commented, “I’m glad you have it, Adam. But really, I didn’t want to sell it. It was so much a part of Father.”

“Sweet music is to be shared, sometimes with many, sometimes with few. There is music which two can share, and there is music to be played by one alone. You have found music in this violin to touch the lonely heart of another. Perhaps I can find that music, too,” was his inscrutable reply.

7

WINTER JOURNEYINGS

"Come see what's turnin' in at the brick house, Jerry." Jeremiah Cobb dropped his *New England Homestead* magazine at his wife's call. He shuffled in his stocking feet to the window where Aunt Sarah Cobb had parted the curtains. He had not seen such a sight since the Simpsons, with their passel of kids, had been sent back to their hometown by the Riverboro selectmen.

An old, high-wheeled hayrack, with baggage and bureaus and bedsteads seeming to reach the gray November skies, groaned and creaked and teetered as it was drawn by the two straining gray mares up the incline from the narrow street. Two young men, silhouetted by the setting sun, clung tenaciously to the top of the heap, the taller one gripping the reins.

"Land o' Goshen," Uncle Jerry exclaimed, diving for his shoes beside his reclining Morris chair, "that must be John and Mark Randall with their mother's stuff at last. They'll put them hosses in Deacon Sawyer's old barn, an' there ain't a mite o' hay in there fit for a beast. Why, if there's enny left, it's all at least twenty years old an' so full o' mold that it'd give 'em the heaves, fer sure."

"We've got some extry in the stable—more'n our horses will eat this winter, I'm sure," Sarah Cobb put in thoughtfully. "Why don't we loan them a wagonload till they can buy some?"

"My sentiments exactly," her husband agreed, lacing his shoes. "My old back won't let me help unload that heavy furniture, but I can pitch a few forkfuls o' that hay into the rear of my buckboard and tote it over there. And I better get goin'; them hosses must be hungry." He grabbed his coat and headed out the back kitchen door toward the stable with an agitated hobble.

To tell the truth, Uncle Jerry Cobb was more than glad to make his appearance at the brick house. Aunt Sarah had gone over with a pie made from her best canned blackberries when Aurelia had arrived with Rebecca, Jenny, and Fanny three days earlier. Rebecca, of course, had been in to call on old Uncle Jerry and Aunt Sarah. There was much hugging and crying and "Praise the Lord" and "Won't that be grand" when Rebecca told how she'd been given the brick house and Sunnybrook had been sold and the whole family was moving to Riverboro.

So Mr. Cobb wanted very much indeed to meet the masculine side of the Randall family, and he was not disappointed. John, handsome like his father, yet tall and muscular as Grandfather Sawyer had been, showed also his French Canadian ancestry with his hair, black and kinky like Rebecca's, Roman nose, and a strong chin. So much a larger copy of his father did he appear, in fact, that Uncle Jerry later told Aunt Sarah that it seemed uncanny to meet a "Frenchman who didn't have a French accent." Mark, though small and wiry like his father, like his mother and his two younger sisters was a true Saxon, with straight, sandy hair and blue eyes that always seemed to be planning merriment.

"Want to sell them hosses, do ye?" Uncle Jerry remarked to John after they had chatted a while. "There's a livestock and feed auction over at the Davis barn on Turner Ridge Road next Saturday. Several farmers are goin' in together, and I wouldn't be surprised but what they'd let you join 'em. You might even find yourself a drivin' hoss to pull that ol' top buggy your grandfather left in the barn, and I'm sure you could get hay enough to keep it 'til spring."

John not only sold his workhorses and the hayrack, but he got money enough for them to buy Molly, a fine, brown-eyed, cream-colored jersey for a family cow. Dapple-gray Dick-Boy, a retired trotter, once the champion of the York County Fair, became the Randall family's first driving horse since their father had died a decade earlier. And three tons of pressed hay, enough to keep the two animals until the pastures greened in May, John had delivered to the barn—all for the price of the team of work horses.

❧ ❧ ❧

Harriet Beecher Stowe had been one of Rebecca's Most Important Maine People for as long as she could remember. She had read and reread *Uncle Tom's Cabin* while still a small girl at Sunnybrook. When Rebecca and Hannah and John had played "Uncle Tom," an old hen coop had been the cabin, and the bean patches and cornfields of Sunnybrook had become the cotton fields and sugar plantations of the Deep South. Hannah, who took Eliza's part, carried across the "Ohio" brook whatever infant she happened to be tending—Mark, Fanny, or Mira. And Rebecca could be as evil a Simon Legree as if Mrs. Stowe herself had created her.

Though Harriet Stowe—unlike Longfellow, another of Rebecca's Chosen Few favorites—had not actually been born in Maine, her ten years in Brunswick, Maine, and her books about the Down East State had firmly fixed her in Rebecca's imagination as a Maine writer.

After the tent play at the fair in Milltown, however, Rebecca first realized that here were real people—albeit portrayed in fiction—acting out real tragedies. Though in her childish way she had continued to act out the play she had watched with Emma Jane Perkins and Uncle Jerry and Aunt Sarah Cobb, she stored in her heart from that time onward a tender compassion awaiting an awakening to human need and misery.

Right after Thanksgiving a letter arrived at the brick house from Miss Emily Maxwell of Wareham Academy inviting Rebecca to join her for several days at Bowdoin College in Brunswick, where they would meet Mrs. Stowe, visiting there to address the students at the same vine-entwined halls in which her husband, the Reverend Calvin Stowe, had once been professor of theology. In her home in the shadows of these same ivy-covered buildings four decades earlier, Mrs. Stowe had written her famous book, which according to President Lincoln had made her the "Little woman who started this great Civil War." So Rebecca felt her heart leap for joy as she read Miss Maxwell's letter.

"Mother! Aunt Jane!" Rebecca shrieked in tones which would surely have shocked dear departed Aunt Miranda. "She's coming! I'm going to meet her at last! We're leaving next week." Her dark eyes shining, she added, "Miss Maxwell says there may be a position for me in Brunswick, to begin right after the holidays in January."

Aurelia, cane in hand, arose from her task of peeling northern spy apples for pies to face Rebecca, who was fairly flying as she ran into the kitchen from the sitting room where she had been reading the mail. "*Who's* coming, Rebecca? And I presume you mean coming to Brunswick?"

Rebecca responded by pushing a *Portland Press-Herald* news clipping into Mother's free hand. Surmounting the news item was a steel-cut photo of Harriet Beecher Stowe. "Mrs. Stowe to Address Bowdoin Students and Faculty; Alumni to Attend," the headline read. Its subtitle was, "*Uncle Tom* Author Will Talk on Improvement for Negro People."

"She is really, truly going to be in Brunswick, Mother. And we are going to *meet* her!"

"In December?" Aunt Jane interrupted. "Couldn't you go durin' the summer? Maybe she'll be back then."

"Oh, Aunt Jane," Rebecca answered condescendingly, "it's hardly an hour, even from Maplewood by train, and we shall ride the coach from our front door right to the depot. We'll be leaving Saturday morning and be back by Tuesday evening. Besides, Mrs. Stowe is past eighty, I'm sure. If she can travel to Maine in winter all the way from her home in Hartford, Connecticut, I guess it won't hurt Emily Maxwell and me to go forty miles to Brunswick!"

"I'd ride horseback to Brunswick in December—I'd walk, even, if I could meet Mrs. Stowe," Aurelia agreed with Rebecca. Like her precocious daughter, Aurelia Randall filled her spare time with reading. Along with their Bible verses and prayers, the Randall children were tucked in each night with the verses of Longfellow or Tennyson or Walter Scott. The tales of Dickens and George MacDonald had carried Aurelia and her children far off to England and Scotland during many a long New England winter evening. And through the imagination of Mrs. Stowe, Aurelia, whose sole experience with Negroes had been to view a black sailor on the streets of Portland some years earlier, had seen Cincinnati and St. Louis and New Orleans.

"Miranda used to blame Lorenzo for Rebecca's flightiness," Jane remarked with restrained amusement. "But it's coming back to me now. You were quite an imp yourself thirty years ago. And when those boys of yours, John an' Mark, pulled in here last week with hosses and a hay wagon full o' baggage an' furniture after three days' travel over frozen ruts and two nights spent sleepin' in barns, why—you acted like there was nothin' to it! You'd have gone with 'em yourself if you hadn't a-been used up so bad from yer fall, I believe."

"It was quite a trip, I'll admit, sister. But it's my thinkin' that's what they needed to make men out of 'em." Aurelia chuckled as Rebecca joined the glee at Aunt Jane's consternation.

"Well, they got here in one piece, that's the important thing," Jane said decidedly. "But, Aurelia, it's December," she added in earnest concern. "A no'theastuh comin' up the coast could leave them stranded in Brunswick for weeks!"

"I guess Rebecca's had about enough independence to know how to take care of herself," Aurelia answered mildly. "Brunswick isn't such a bad place to be stranded, anyway—what with several hundred young college fellows around, I'm sure the girls will do just fine," she joked.

"Auntie," Rebecca added earnestly, "Miss Maxwell said in her letter that there's a wonderful position open in Brunswick, but if I'm to have it, I need to go at once for an interview. The Deering Oaks Preparatory School wants a piano teacher, since theirs is leaving at Christmastime to get married. Now that Mother is here at the brick house and on the mend, I can pursue a career."

"Tell us more about it, Becky dear." Aurelia hung up her cane and sat down at the kitchen table.

Rebecca joined Aurelia at the table, and Jane sat down as well.

"Deering Oaks is a prep school for Bowdoin College," told Rebecca with apparent amusement. "The sons and daughters of the well-to-do from Brunswick and Portland—some from Boston, even, go there to 'finish' their education or to make up deficiencies they need to get into college."

"Well, you certainly must be very happy for such an opportunity. Your Aunt Miranda would be proud of you," Aunt Jane answered, almost in awe.

"Yes," said Aurelia. "We are proud, too. But do I detect some merriment in your voice? What's the joke?"

"To think—Abijah Flagg is a Bowdoin student!" Rebecca exclaimed. "I was his prep school, his common school, even! I wonder why some young people need extra education to succeed? Others, whom you'd think couldn't amount to anything, seem to soar like eagles with just a little help."

Aurelia's eyes moistened as she listened to her daughter's lilting query. "Rebecca, honey," she said, using an endearing term she reserved for times of warmest emotion, "my heart ached so very, very much when you left Sunnybrook to live with your aunts. Oh, I tried to be brave and to remind you to mind your manners, and such."

"It *is* a journey when you carry a nightgown, Mother," Rebecca gleefully reminisced. Mother and daughter laughed together as Aunt Jane smiled in polite incomprehension.

"And when you came home for Mira's funeral, only to leave again, it 'most tore my heart out," Aurelia went on. "While I firmly believe that in the natural, normal state of things it is God's will for children to be raised by their own parents, sometimes the Lord has plans that are better for us. Storms toughen oaks, and people, too. I have hopes that like Abijah you also will join the eagles!"

"Aunt Jane and Aunt Miranda were *my* preparatory school, I guess," concluded Rebecca.

❧ ❧ ❧

Leaden skies and not a breath of breeze greeted Rebecca and Emily Maxwell the second Saturday in December as the old Concord coach, once the pride of Jeremiah Cobb, drew up to the brick house's front entrance, its leather springs creaking in the bitter cold. It was midmorning; the young ladies were thankful, at least, that the stage left late on Saturday, for at breakfast time the thermometer on the back porch had stood at ten degrees below zero. Now, two hours later, it was only ten above, and the ride in the drafty, unheated coach would be endured only as a necessary means to reach the Saco & Androscoggin River Railroad depot in Maplewood.

Miss Maxwell had ridden to Riverboro from Wareham the day before with friends who had to catch a Friday train to Portland. She was no stranger to the brick house; since Riverboro lies between Wareham and Portland, on several occasions she had paused there on her trips to the city to report to the aunts how the "old maids' child" was progressing in school.

By the time the coach reached Maplewood in mid-afternoon, heavy snow had begun to drift across the frozen ruts of the gravel road. The driver had slowed his horses to a walk for the last couple of miles, and on several occasions he had braked on a downgrade to keep the coach from running ahead on the horses, causing them to loose their footing.

Grumbling about needing to get back to Riverboro "before this blizzard sets in a grand style," the driver hastily threw the passengers' bags on the railway platform. His sole return passenger jumped aboard, and he wheeled his horses about and slapped the reins. By the time Rebccca and Emily were inside the depot, the coach was out of sight in a swirl of snow.

"We've got plenty of time, Rebecca," Emily said as they studied the chalkboard timetable in the tiny depot of the Saco & Androscoggin. Departure was at 3:30 P.M., and arrival in Brunswick was just an hour and a half later, even with five stops between. The stationmaster had assured them that his telegraph reported that the eastbound train was on schedule—"Keeping just ahead of the eye of the storm," he remarked. So the young women settled in to eat their sandwiches by the depot's potbellied stove.

Once the train arrived, Rebecca and Emily found the passenger cars on the narrow-gauge railway, like the depot, passably cozy. Though icy blasts from the door opening and closing as passengers entered and disembarked sent chills around Rebecca's ankles, the warmth from the car's coal stove comforted her. Comforting, too, was the thought that at last they were on their way to meet her heroine. The train finally began to move, and through the gathering dusk of the early evening, Rebecca saw the oil-lit windows of Maplewood's three dozen village homes slide past the train. Soon they were rolling through the hills, barren now, except for clumps of pine forest and the ubiquitous stone walls which lace every Maine hillside and hollow.

"May I borrow your watch, please?" Rebecca asked, an idea grabbing her as a granite milepost passed their window. The lonely whistle of the steam boiler carried back from the locomotive ahead to signal the last crossing outside Maplewood, breaking the monotony of the "click-clack, click-clack" of the wheels on the rails.

Rebecca took note of the watch's second hand as they passed another milepost. She watched the hand mark a minute, then two, while she strained to see the number on the next post in the dying rays of the sun, now fast dropping behind the White Mountains behind them in New Hampshire. She had almost given up when she spied the post; checking Emily's watch, she noted that almost exactly three minutes had passed.

"Twenty miles an hour," Rebecca grumbled, passing Emily her watch with its silver chain. Worried, she recalled that the Temperance train topped forty on the straight stretches and even rounded the bends at thirty. "Will we be in time to hear Mrs. Stowe's speech?" Rebecca worried aloud.

"I'm sure we will," Miss Maxwell answered confidently, pinning her watch chain back in place with a brooch and dropping the dainty timepiece into her breast pocket. Noting Rebecca's consternation, she pulled out the engraved invitation for the evening meeting, addressed to "Bowdoin Alumni and Guests." "She will speak at 7:30," Emily noted. "Even at this rate we'll be in Brunswick in time to take a hansom cab to Cap'n Cates' Chowder House, next to the campus, and eat a leisurely meal before strolling over to the chapel. Since I have already paid in advance for our room at the Brunswick Inn, we can just hang onto our valises until after the meeting."

8

MRS. STOWE OF BOWDOIN COLLEGE

As evening descended on the little steam train, Rebecca watched the farmhouses vanish in the swirling snow. Once on a bend she saw the glimmer of the engine's single, sputtering carbide lamp against an ice-covered rock cut. As the locomotive plunged into a drift, the snow flew high, then the train was swallowed again in the wild night. Rebecca had the sensation of being entombed in a moving vault, lighted within only by the dim glow of kerosene lamps.

On into the night the little train with its anxious passengers rumbled. Though little more than an hour had passed during the short run to Brunswick, it seemed an eternity to Rebecca, so intent on reaching Bowdoin's chapel that each interminable stop seemed to last forever. Then she felt the cars slow, then shudder, then stop. Presently the conductor appeared. "Locomotive's hopped the rails," was his taciturn report.

Rebecca stood at once, as Emily tried in vain to restrain her. "Sir," she said urgently, "we must get to Bowdoin College by half past seven!"

"We ain't got no snowshoes on this train, miss. That's what you'll need if you're goin' to Brunswick tonight."

"Where are we?" Emily put in.

"Johnson's Crossin'—four miles to the station, yet. It's only a derailment. Lucky we didn't land in the river."

Through the night Rebecca slept fitfully in her iron-framed leather seat. Fortunately, the Saturday evening run had been nearly empty, so only two other passengers, besides herself and Emily, shared their car, and the other cars were also nearly empty. Her body was aching and sore—how she envied Jacob and his pillow of stone! Twice she awoke with a start as the conductor rattled the grate of the coal heater at the end of the car.

"Mornin', miss. We have hot tea," was the conductor's laconic announcement, which finally stirred Rebecca fully awake. Sunday had dawned bright since the storm had passed. It was a quarter past seven, and the Androscoggin River gleamed like amber glass in the sun where the wind had swept the ice bare.

Rebecca sat up, irritated at being interrupted when she had at last fallen asleep. "Yes, I'll have some, please," she murmured sleepily.

"Better get your wraps and galoshes on," the conductor advised brusquely. "There's a span o' hosses haulin' a four-seat sleigh on the ice below us. They're here to take us into Brunswick. Got room for twelve!"

"How about the roads?" Rebecca knew that the question was pointless as soon as she had uttered it.

"Fireman says the roads are plugged solid. Nawthin's movin'. Fireman walked to a farmhouse to phone for help at five o'clock, soon's the farmer lit his lantern to milk his cows."

"But . . . but the train!" Remembering their missed meeting with Mrs. Stowe, it seemed to Rebecca that Aunt Jane's prophecy was about to come true.

"Section gang's on the way, already," replied the conductor. "Should have 'er movin' in six, eight hours, I figguh."

Twelve places, it turned out, was just enough space in the rescue sleigh for the train's passengers, except for the engineer and the fireman, who stayed with the locomotive awaiting the arrival of the repair crew by hand car. Four women, including Rebecca and Emily, had spent the night in the forward car, and six men, besides the conductor, did their best to stay comfortable in the rear. The four seats on the two-horse sleigh, would seat three passengers each, wedged tightly together under buffalo-skin robes.

As the girls stepped into the open air, Rebecca drew a deep breath, glad to be out of the sooty, acrid atmosphere of the car with its coal stove and oil lamps. The sharp bite of the morning chill on the tender linings of her nostrils warned Rebecca that the storm had been replaced by an Arctic chill far below zero which would frost her lungs if she exerted herself and breathed too deeply.

The ten passengers followed the conductor Indian-file through the drifts toward the head of the train. "Watch them tubes—they're hot!" the conductor brusquely commented, as they reached the locomotive. The fireman had kept a slow fire in the boiler all night to keep the tubes from freezing, and live steam hissed even then from relief valves.

At the river embankment leading to the ice, Rebecca saw at once that the rails ran on stone slabs, laid up like stairs from the water's edge, making an easy, though steep, climb down for the nimble and agile. At the bottom of the descent was parked a heavy sleigh, painted dull green, with "S. & A. R. R. R." in gold letters across the back.

The driver, an unambitious youth wearing a mackinaw and stocking cap, sat dangling one leg over the ice from the front seat as he puffed lazily on his pipe.

The conductor paused by the stone ladder, then perfunctorily took a valise from a richly dressed lady in front of Rebecca and started down without offering her his elbow. "I . . . can't . . . go . . . a . . . single . . . step . . . further," came the almost inaudible voice of the frail-appearing, thin elderly lady swaddled in mink directly in front of Rebecca.

"May we help, ma'am?" Rebecca offered at once, taking her elbow.

"Yes, let us." It was Emily, close behind.

Rebecca glared for a second at the young sleigh driver, who unmoving, viewed the episode with what seemed to Rebecca contemptuous amusement. The conductor himself had by now placed the lady's valise, along with his own, under a seat. But though he had begun to shuffle back toward the stone steps, Rebecca could see that, old and none too agile, his help in the situation would be mostly symbolic.

"Catch!" she cried impetuously, flinging her own cheap carpetbag valise across the ice at the sleigh driver. Whether to avoid catching it in the face from Rebecca's accurate pitch or to be helpful, he caught the bag and stashed it away without comment.

"Sit down—we'll carry you," Emily Maxwell urged the lady gently as she grasped Rebecca's arms, forming a cradle.

"But . . . but what if you girls should fall?"

"I wouldn't say you had any choice, lady," impatiently insisted a portly, opulently dressed, though rumpled businessman behind Rebecca, who had been eyeing the proceedings in irritation. "If that sleigh driver'd get off his seat and help the women," he raved on, "we'd be on our way. The railroad must think we want to spend the week-end ice fishing!" The talkative gentleman, in fur-trimmed cashmere overcoat and silk hat with fur earmuffs, carried only a thin briefcase in one kid-gloved hand. His other hand in Napoleonic fashion, was rammed lazily inside his warm coat.

"Just a minute, Emily." Rebecca released her grip on Emily's arms, retrieved Emily's valise from the locomotive cowcatcher where she had stashed it, intending to return for it. "Here—make yourself useful, mister!" Rebecca rammed the heavy leather valise into the man's unready ribs so forcefully that its brass corner made him wince in pain. Turning back to Emily and the old lady, she repositioned herself with Emily to form a cradle. "Let's go! Ready?" Without waiting for a reply, Rebecca started down and Emily walked in step. They nimbly navigated the steep granite steps and deposited their passenger safely in the sleigh's second seat, seating themselves beside her.

Twenty minutes later the sleigh lurched up the riverbank over a steep path where in summer cattle came to drink just outside the city. Soon they drew up at the station, and the conductor explained that anyone not waiting a through train to Augusta would be driven to a hotel, courtesy of the railway. "The Brunswick Inn, please," Miss Maxwell replied. Without a word the driver slapped the reins, and inside of five minutes he deposited the young ladies at their hotel.

"I guess we've missed Mrs. Stowe," Rebecca remarked glumly, as later she and Emily washed in the bathroom just down the hall from their room. "But I'm sure that the Lord is in this. For some reason He wanted us to miss that meeting last night."

"Is that faith or fatalism?" queried Emily lightly.

"I'm afraid my faith is rather thin right now," Rebecca admitted; and after a pause, "Where do we go from here?"

"Soon's we freshen up and replace these rumpled blouses with pressed ones, I vote for ham and potatoes in the hotel dining room. Or you could have corned beef hash, or eggs and bacon, or fried hasty pudding. If you insist on a traditional Maine Sunday country breakfast, I'm sure they have warmed-over Saturday night's baked yelloweyed beans," Emily responded in forced merriment. "Then there's plenty of time to make the eleven o'clock at the First Parish Church."

"I think I'd love to live in Brunswick," Rebecca glowed later over their ham and fried potatoes. "From what I saw from the sleigh and our hotel window, it seems like such a romantic city."

"Bowdoin College *does* have a beautiful campus," affirmed Miss Maxwell.

"Yes! Did you notice how the rugged winter beauty of those graceful, bare, wine-glass-shaped elms is set off so gorgeously by the tall green pines here and there across the campus and on into the residential neighborhoods, also? And those ivy-covered halls!"

"Have you forgotten I spent three years here before going to Wareham to teach?" Emily raised an eyebrow.

"No, no, I haven't. But how else am I going to express myself about all this beauty if I don't tell *someone* about it?" Rebecca said in mock childish tones. Then changing to adult seriousness, "Oh, Emily, to meet Harriet Beecher Stowe is why I *really* came to Brunswick. Do you think she's gone back to Hartford?"

"No. I expect she'll stay 'til tomorrow, at least. No doubt she has old friends she wishes to call on."

"Then . . . then isn't there some way we could meet her?"

"I wish I knew how. I hear she's a very private person. Last night was her first lecture in more than a dozen years, and she did that only for a select audience. We got invitations only because I am a Bowdoin alumna. But after your interview at Deering Oaks tomorrow, I'll ask around."

"Promise?"

"Promise!"

An hour later, Rebecca and Emily were ushered to a seat about halfway down the aisle of First Parish Church, just as another usher was seating a well-dressed elderly lady in a front pew. Though Rebecca could not see the woman's face since it was shaded by the brim of her old-fashioned bonnet, she noticed curls of steel-gray hair poking out here and there. The lady's dress was of heavily brocaded, layered, black silk, and she wore an elegant gray alpaca shawl which matched her knit silk gloves.

After the service, Rebecca, who had an aisle seat, politely waited for the press of people passing down the aisle to pass her before venturing into the throng. She caught sight of the black silk skirt and the tiny woman who wore it, though her face was hidden by a gentleman just a step ahead of her.

The man courteously stepped aside to let the lady pass just as Rebecca glanced toward the front of the church. She unintentionally peered directly into the lady's face, and suddenly remembering the photo in the *Press-Herald* she'd seen a week earlier, gasped, "Mrs. Stowe!"

"Yes, I'm Hattie Stowe," the lady acknowledged, smiling disarmingly. "Is it possible that we've met?" The lady's tone of voice betrayed to Rebecca more than mere polite friendliness.

"I'm sorry," Rebecca began to apologize. "I didn't mean to . . . oh!" Rebecca blushed uncontrollably. "You're . . . I mean we . . .we carried you to the sleigh this morning!"

"You did indeed, and I'm grateful beyond words. Did you come for the lecture? I'm afraid in last night's storm the attendance would have been sorry, to say the least. But where are you from?"

"Riverboro. And this is Miss Emily Maxwell, a Bowdoin alumna and my former teacher at Wareham."

"Oh, you ladies have come such a long way! And there was no meeting. But I've had other inconveniences, as well. I was to dine after church today with Professor and Mrs. Ashcroft, but I received a note just before the service that the Ashcrofts are both ill with the flu. Dear old Doctor Wilberson, who arranged my itinerary here, is right now trying to buttonhole some hapless parishioner in the foyer to take a half-addled old lady out to lunch, I'm afraid. I'll tell him I have two charming young ladies as *my* guests, and we shall dine together at Cap'n Cates' Chowder House." Silk skirts swishing, Mrs. Stowe bustled down the aisle. Rebecca and Emily, embarrassed yet pleased, followed a respectful distance behind.

"My big mouth!" Rebecca moaned to Emily, as Mrs. Stowe, getting into her fur coat, explained the change in plans to Professor Wilberson, a worried-looking little man in spats, tweeds, and horn-rimmed glasses.

"Your big mouth has just got us a private audience with the leading lady of American letters, Becky dear," Emily answered in hushed awe.

❧ ❧ ❧

"Rebecca was telling me on the train yesterday how much she loves *Uncle Tom's Cabin,* so much, even, that she and her brothers and sisters used to act it out time and time again when they were children," Miss Maxwell explained to

Mrs. Stowe while they were waiting for their bowls of steaming clam chowder later at Cates'.

Rebecca, embarrassed at losing her composure on meeting 'Hattie' Stowe face-to-face, had said little for some moments. Earnestly she now inquired, "Mrs. Stowe, why did you write that book? Did it come as a sudden inspiration?"

"My father, Reverend Lyman Beecher, was a preacher of the old Puritan gospel and also a warrior against the abuse of liquor," she explained quietly. "I learned early in my life from his example to do battle where the fight is the thickest and not back down. But I was thrown into the middle of the anti-slavery fight more than fifty years ago when I lived in Cincinnati. From there I traveled just across the river into Kentucky and saw the degradation of human beings who were owned like animals by other human beings. And I saw the fright and fear on faces of escaped slaves who came north across the Ohio River on their way to freedom in Canada, fleeing the bounty hunters.

"Then one day in 1837 the news came that my brother Edward, who had gone to St. Louis to help a young circuit-riding preacher, Elijah Lovejoy, had been murdered by a pro-slavery mob in Alton, Illinois, across the river from St. Louis, when he was protecting Mr. Lovejoy's printing press. Though we learned weeks later that Edward was really alive and unharmed, the report that Lovejoy had in fact been murdered for printing stories opposing slavery, and had left his ill wife and an infant son without a husband and father, tore deeply into my heart," Mrs. Stowe explained.

"I have certainly heard of Elijah Parish Lovejoy," said Rebecca, her eyes aglow. "He was born in Albion, not a hundred miles from here. But Mrs. Stowe, there are so many causes, so many tasks for a young person such as myself to choose among—how does one know what to do with one's life?" Rebecca besought the great lady.

"Many people drift through their whole lives because they have never squarely faced this question." Mrs. Stowe grew quiet and somber, yet her eyes twinkled with delight as she answered. "Do what you *must* do," she said. "If you can easily get out of a course of life, it's not for you. The same goes for marriage—never marry a man until you find it impossible to live without him. If there are other choices—another man, spinsterhood—you're not ready for marriage. If God impresses on your mind and heart that He has a task you may not escape, a course of action your heart will not permit you to avoid, then that is what you must do, no matter what.

"Put your hand to the plow and never look back. My dear father believed that our destinies were planned in the mind of God millennia before we were created, but that some miss God's will for their lives because they choose the easy road rather than the right road. Those who thus choose the easy way, like Bunyan's distracted Pilgrim, wander in their Bypass Meadows, never plowing their furrows, never planting, never reaping. If you stay determinedly on the high road, you'll not be sorry, nor have I ever been sorry."

❧ ❧ ❧

Tuesday came, and Rebecca and Emily rode together in the morning on the little Saco & Androscoggin River train, which pushed westward across the frozen farmlands toward Maplewood, where Rebecca would catch the stage back to Riverboro and Emily would catch another train back to Wareham and the academy. Rebecca withdrew a sheaf of important-looking papers from an inside pocket of her long winter overcoat and read them for the fourth time, or the fifth—she didn't recall which.

The Monday interview at Deering Oaks Preparatory School had gone very well indeed. Besides a position as a piano and voice instructor, the school offered—no, insisted—that she take evening classes twice weekly at their expense at Bowdoin toward a degree. Her record at Wareham had impressed Deering's directors, and with Miss Maxwell present as a reference, Rebecca had been offered a contract at once.

Rebecca perused the contract papers. Seven dollars a week, it stipulated, in addition to a private room in the prep school girls' dorm and meals in the school dining hall. She was expected to put in seven daytime hours with piano and voice students in the conservatory, plus two evenings a week from seven until ten o'clock. On her free evening from classes at Bowdoin or Deering, she was, of course, expected to attend prayer meeting at a church of the orthodox faith. She was to receive one month's vacation with pay.

The contract was dated December 15, 1893, Monday. She had seven days, until December 22, to accept or decline the offer, and a stamped envelope had thoughtfully been provided for her response. Rebecca returned the contract to its envelope, then shoved it inside her coat, in the pocket over her heart.

But Rebecca's heart was troubled as she dozed off to the clickety-clack of the train's wheels. How would she be doing a service for mankind by giving private piano lessons to the spoiled scions of rich Bostonians, many of whom hadn't thought enough of their high school or academy education to pass Latin and algebra and history with a score satisfactory to enter college. True, the free classes at

Bowdoin were an incentive. It was an opportunity which surely would be envied, Rebecca knew, by girls like herself across Maine who each day rang their brass bells for the two or three dozen urchins, washed and unwashed, who resorted to the one-room schools which smelled of oiled maple floors, chalk dust, and wood smoke.

Abijah Flagg came to mind as Rebecca thought on these things. She recalled the bits and pieces of news of Abijah's mercurial progress at Bowdoin fed her by Emma Jane Perkins from time to time. How she had longed to drop in on Abijah and surprise him with a visit while in Brunswick, but because of their tight schedule and questions of propriety at inviting herself into his presence, she had decided against it.

Rebecca smiled and laughed aloud in her nap as she thought on Abijah. She rested now, at peace with herself.

At the Maplewood depot, both young women found they had some minutes before their coaches—rail and horse-drawn—pulled out for their respective villages. Rebecca stashed her valise on the Riverboro coach, then, "I've got some business at the post office," she told Emily. Across the street she unfolded the contract on the post office writing stand. Drawing a pen from its inkwell, she wrote across the top with a smooth, steady hand:

> Your kindness in granting me an interview is much appreciated. I must decline the offer of a position at Deering, however, since it is not what I believe the Lord would have me do.
>
> Yours,
> Rebecca R. Randall

Rebecca slipped the contract into the return-address envelope, raised the brass door on the mail slot, and dropped it in.

"Miss Randall?" It was the Riverboro coach driver, emerging from the cage in the post office with a leather bag across his arm. "I spotted you out here as I was bagging the mail—thought I'd save you a trip to the Riverboro post office."

He passed Rebecca a long, white envelope. *Maine Home for Little Wayfarers, Munjoy Hill, Portland, Maine,* read the return address.

9

THE BRICK HOUSE GETS A CHRISTMAS TREE

The Saturday following Rebecca's trip to Bowdoin College with Miss Maxwell found her brothers, Mark and John Randall, in a holiday mood. Seventeen-year-old John had taken a temporary job, replacing Abijah Flagg as Squire Bean's hired man, since it would be next fall before he could enter Bowdoin to prepare for medical college. And Mark, fourteen, with sister Fanny, twelve, was a student at the village school. Jenny, now fifteen, would take the year off school, and Rebecca would tutor her for Wareham's entrance exams next fall. All, however, had Saturday at home, and they set out to make Christmas at the brick house a Christmas to remember.

Great-grandfather Sawyer had built his modest brick mansion in the grand Federal style, so popular in the early days of the American republic. Though the twelve-foot-high main floor ceilings had made the manse hard to heat through Maine winters—until Deacon Israel Sawyer installed Franklin stoves in all the brick fireplaces right after the Civil War—the house's spacious rooms encouraged a high-spirited holiday season indeed.

With the upstairs bedrooms in use by the addition of Aurelia Randall's Sunnybrook brood to the once-tiny household, three of the four stoves now had to be kept fired up with wood from breakfast until bedtime.

That morning shortly before Christmas, Mark discovered the ponderous, paneled oak doors, which for some twenty years had remained shut, separating the sitting room from the parlor. This necessitated a circuitous trip through the front hall to reach that cavernous room kept sacred in Aunt Miranda's time for funerals and weddings. And that parlor had been used exactly twice in twenty years—once for Deacon Israel's funeral, and once for his daughter, Miranda's.

These decorative panels, Mark realized suddenly, as he fueled the sitting room stove after breakfast, were actually doors designed to slide on rollers and disappear into the plastered walls. Wonderingly, cautiously, he lifted aside the horsehair-upholstered loveseat which had stood against the massive panels since before his memory of the brick house began. Carefully, using a chair as a ladder, he then took down an old portrait of Grandfather and Grandmother Sawyer, which hung in its ornate gold-leaf frame on a wire suspended from a porcelain knob screwed into the crown molding next to the ceiling. Sure enough, a floor-to-ceiling vertical separation in the woodwork seemed to indicate that the panels might be more than mere decoration.

Mark slipped through the hallway to the parlor, where sat the Sawyer "best" furniture, shrouded in old bedsheets which were laundered twice yearly. Cautiously entering the parlor, he drew the hall door silently shut behind him.

A large, glass-doored sectional maple veneer bookcase stood against the far wall, in front of the oak panels. Rebecca had introduced Mark to that case in the weeks since her family had moved into the brick house. Among the good deacon's collection—Foxe's *Martyrs,* works by the Puritan divines, Gibbon's histories, Whiston's translation of Josephus, Weems' *Washington,* works in Latin, and works translated from that moldy tongue—Rebecca had found a full set of Sir Walter Scott's writings, and among them *Ivanhoe,* in which she had discovered her own namesakes, the Misses Rebecca and Rowena.

On many nights Rebecca had selected a volume of what Aunt Miranda had termed "improvin' litterture." After the supper dishes were dried and the last junk of split rock maple had gone into the cast-iron heater in the sitting room, she had curled up on the old leather ottoman with a book until the stove's warmth had receded deep within its metal bowels, and she was forced to carry her lamp to her cold chamber upstairs in the kitchen ell. There, snug in flannel sheets, she would read by the light on her lampstand until she could no longer hold her eyelids up.

Mark, too, had learned these pleasures from Rebecca, whose education at Wareham Academy had done nothing to diminish her craving for the late-night reverie of a good novel or book of poems.

Now, though, Mark found in these books a new challenge. If Aunt Jane, or even his mother, discovered him at his deed, they might command him sternly to stop. And with several siblings who might at any moment be roaming the house, Mark had reason enough to fear discovery. He knew, though, that Jenny and Fanny had gone together over to Watson's Mercantile for a sack of sugar, and Rebecca was helping her elders with the after-breakfast chores. Though she was now mistress of the manor, Rebecca, mindful of her youth, ordinarily demurred to her elders when it came to domestic duties.

So, fairly jumping with the excitement of what he was about to accomplish, Mark hurriedly began to unload the bookcase onto the Persian carpet. The top section he emptied and set aside. Then the second. By then he discovered that the case could now be pushed aside. Behind the bookcase, Mark was happy to spy a brass catch set into the beam supporting one section of the paneling, accessible only from the parlor side. He pushed the catch firmly with his thumb, and it slid stiffly in its slot to release the panels.

But try as he might, Mark could not get his fingers into the groove between the panels far enough to pull. Then an idea struck him. He drew aside the drapes covering the parlor's tall east window. The December morning sun's rays slanting brightly from the southeast poured in, and the pallor of the cavernous old parlor was dispelled. Plainly now, though green with corrosion from its years behind the bookcase, a brass handle set flush with the woodwork appeared. Mark pressed a button set beside the handle, and the handle popped forth, furnishing a firm hand hold. He pulled, and to his satisfaction the door rolled easily into the wall. A push in the other direction, and the door's mate disappeared, also sliding silently into its hiding place between the walls.

Mark strode through the grand opening he had created, delighted at once that the spacious parlor was now one room with the smaller sitting room. He walked to the hall door for a fuller view. Pleased with the effect, he called, "Ma! Aunt Jane! Becky! Come see!"

"I don't know," was Jane Sawyer's worried plaint, as moments later she stood with Aurelia and Rebecca beside Mark, Aurelia bending over her cane.

"Father *always* opened up both rooms for the holidays," put in Aurelia, defending Mark. She, too, was delighted with the effect, and she scarcely could suppress her elation.

"I like it," Rebecca said decidedly.

"It's your house, now, of course, Rebecca," cautiously worried Jane. "But when your Grandfather Sawyer was alive, the woodshed'd be filled to the rafters with firewood each fall, so's we could *afford* t' heat the hull house if we wanted to. But now with the upstairs opened up an' all the stoves goin', we're going to have to buy more wood by February as it is—havin' only begun the winter with the three cords of hardwood Miranda 'n' I usually use, besides a wagon load o' pine sawmill edgings fer kindlin'. The parlor stove'll take a lot o' wood."

"I guess you're right, Auntie," Rebecca answered, plainly disappointed. "I hadn't thought of that."

"Nonsense," objected Aurelia firmly but mildly. "We sold all our firewood before we left Sunnybrook, so it's only right that we spend the money to buy fuel to heat this house. You're right, it's too late t' get anything but green wood, so I'll order a ton o' coal from the grocer. He takes orders for the Portland Coal and Ice Co., don't he?"

"He surely does," affirmed Jane. Secretly, she believed buying coal from the city to be an extravagance. Her mind ran on the hundreds of acres of woodlands she herself owned, and how over the years she had kept the house supplied with winter fuel by making deals with villagers who needed firewood, but who owned no timber of their own. Even now, a crew of loggers was cutting the pine and spruce and hemlock sawlogs on one of her lots, stacking aside the birch, beech, oak, and maple for firewood. But it would be another fall, she knew, before that cutting of cordwood would be dry enough to summon Jeremiah Cobb to haul it into the woodshed with his dray wagon and coach horses.

Jane's heart, however, sang a more melodious song then did her head. Deep within, she felt that Aurelia and

Rebecca were right. Why should the family exist in tight-fisted penury when they had been blessed with money enough and to spare? If the ample life-style of an earlier generation of Sawyers was to express itself once more at the brick house, she would not object.

John, now in from cleaning up his grandfather's dusty old sleigh in the barn, joined the group in the sitting room. "Why . . . why it's almost like a ballroom," he exclaimed. "And we could put our Christmas tree against that tall window," he said, indicating the window with the open drapes, which reached almost to the high ceiling.

John and Mark, who had each December procured a small balsam fir from beside the brook to grace the sitting room at Sunnybrook, soon hurried off—one carrying an ax, the other a light bucksaw—to seek out a far more magnificent model for the brick house's parlor. Sunnybrook's Cape Cod cottage had a low, seven-foot ceiling, but for the brick house they must discover a much grander tree. Though their mother had advised them that even Deacon Sawyer would not have done so, they determined to have a tree which reached the high ceiling.

It was a hope-filled, joyous procession that plodded over the crusted snow across the fields below the brick house and its barn that Saturday forenoon shortly before Christmas. John led the way toward a clump of firs in the distance, which for some days he had been eyeing from his upstairs bedroom window as a likely spot to find a suitable tree. He urged tag-along Fanny to hurry up, pointing with his ax handle toward the tallest fir within this thicket on a rocky bluff across the frozen Saco. "We'll cross the river on the ice, cut her, and drag 'er back. That's *our* tree fer shore," he assured his three sisters. "We'll have it home in time fer noon dinner."

Ted Perkins's long-legged tri-colored hound . . . raced joyfully ahead or bayed madly after a snowshoe hare.

"It looks awful big," complained Fanny, who moments earlier had been grumbling about scraping her wrists raw and bruising her face bloody on snow crusted from a sleet storm days earlier. Frequent falls had taken their toll. Rebecca and Jenny had time and time again helped the smaller sister to her feet, Rebecca wiping snow from Fanny's eyes, and Jenny dabbing with her handkerchief the blood from her sister's spindly wrists which had been rammed roughly through the crust. Yet, pleased by the prospect of such a marvelous tree to celebrate their first Christmas in the brick house, the brave group plodded on. Old Bowser, Emma and Ted Perkins's long-legged tri-colored hound, who, now that his master and mistress were grown spent his days with Mark at the brick house, raced joyfully ahead or bayed madly after a snowshoe hare. Then ears flapping, he circled back to trot and sniff at their heels.

It was near noon when the party mounted the bluff and arrived at the base of the fir. The tree, indeed, was tall—much taller than they expected. Though as perfect in symmetry as any fir which ever grew in a tannenbaum thicket, it had been spared the axes of yuletide revelers over the years by having grown on a nearly insurmountable cliff which had successfully intimidated tree choppers of lesser valor.

The tree, in fact, towered more than thirty feet above the promontory. The young people's argument that this was *their* tree, spotted from the brick house, and destined for their parlor, soon won out over Rebecca's concern about cutting such a huge tree to salvage only a twelve-foot section of top. Mark softened his big sister by promising to saw the left over piece into firewood and later tote it to the house on a toboggan so nothing would be wasted, while John set to work on the trunk with his ax.

A mile and a half is a long way to drag a Christmas tree in deep snow, the merry youths discovered, even using the rope Rebecca had thoughtfully carried from the barn. There were tears from small Fanny, struggles by the brothers, more scrapes and bruises together with laughter, brought the tree across the broad, frozen river-bottom meadows, through the pasture bars in the stone wall, then up the long hill to where the brick house commanded the head of Riverboro Village.

Such a mess the parlor had not seen in many a year! Snow mingled with fir needles was scattered across the floor beginning at the granite front steps, down the hall, and through the sitting room. Here Aunt Jane Sawyer forgot for a moment that she was no longer the mistress of the house. With a "Stop where you are," spoken as sternly as if Aunt Miranda had commanded from her grave, she halted the Christmas tree crew until Rebecca and John could help her roll the parlor carpet aside.

Aurelia, overcome temporarily by her sister's common sense, produced a dressmaker's tape from her sewing bag and measured the tree. "Thirteen feet, eight inches," she announced decidedly. "A couple of feet has to come off."

"Back outside, then!" cried Rebecca, catching the spirit of orderliness which had, for the time being, taken over.

"More snow in the house," moaned Jane in unaccustomed pessimism.

"Then I'll cut it off right here in the sittin' room," John said, taking charge of the situation. Mark dove for the door to fetch his brother the saw. "A little sawdust will be a whole lot less mess than more snow and loose needles," John observed as he waited. Quickly the job was done, and the tree was soon up by the sunny window. Jane's efficient broom brushed the needles and snow out the door, and at Rebecca's request, Mark lugged the stepladder in from the shed as John rolled out the carpet. Rebecca mounted the ladder with the tinsel star, which Jane affirmed had graced every tree in the brick house since her girlhood. The old star soon shone higher in its plastered firmament than ever it had before.

The boys, pleased with their morning's work, left their sisters to deck the tree with the best of what decorations had been brought from Sunnybrook, added to the Sawyer cache of crystal ornaments from their bed of cotton batting in the guest room's dresser drawer. John and Mark now slipped off to the barn for more masculine pursuits.

After breakfast earlier, John had dragged Grandfather Sawyer's old sleigh from where it had rested beneath its dust cloth under a hay scaffold into the light of the window above the barn's front doors. He and Mark now set to work with sandpaper to remove the rust from the runners and polish smooth the rough and loose spots in the old varnish. After repeatedly waxing the runners with paraffin, they set the light cutter on a pair of skids and went to work with varnish and paintbrushes. "Almost as good as new," John decided at last. Pausing only to give their driving horse a scoop of oats and a forkful of hay, the boys walked through the long shed into the house, where the odor of beef stew bubbling on the stove for the noon lunch mingled with that of the yelloweyed beans baking in the oven for supper. Only their determination to see what their sisters had done with the tree got them through the kitchen with its tantalizing odors and into the parlor beyond the sitting room.

The tree, at Rebecca's direction, was now decked with a perfect medley of the handmade ornaments from Sunnybrook and the brick house's heirlooms. It was a magnificent sight! The Christmas of 1893 promised to be the grandest one Riverboro had ever seen.

10

THE SLEIGH RIDE

Night falls early on a New England Christmas Eve, so the evening stars witnessed Rebecca, Aunt Jane, Jenny, and Fanny riding in Grandfather Sawyer's one-horse open sleigh to the five o'clock vesper service at Tory Hill Meeting House. Aunt Sarah Cobb, knowing that the brick house's conveyance was too small to carry the family, had phoned in midafternoon, offering to let Jane Sawyer and Aurelia Randall ride along in their two-seater, which Uncle Jerry Cobb drew with his coach horses in snowy weather. "After all these years carryin' you an' Miranda t' church, it'll only seem natural t' hev your other sister along instead," Aunt Sarah had pleasantly remarked. "The boys kin stand on our sleigh's runnin' boards, so's they won't be crowdin' Rebecca 'n' the two girls in your one-seater."

But as things turned out, Mark left early to walk Thirza Meserve to church. At thirteen Thirza was fast becoming as attractive as her big sister, Huldah, Rebecca noticed uncomfortably. And like Huldah, Thirza set her coy little traps to catch as many unwary fish as possible.

By the time the Cobbs arrived, however, Aunt Jane had broken the string on her best beads, and it would evidently be some moments before she could be ready. "Tell your ma to take John in my place," Jane had instructed Rebecca, who was on her way downstairs to explain the delay.

A one-horse sleigh will carry passengers piled to the stars. So when Aunt Jane was finally ready, Rebecca held the reins on Dick-Boy while Aunt Jane climbed aboard. Jenny squeezed in next, then Fanny piled on Jenny's lap.

The church was aglow with excitement as Rebecca and her family crowded into the old straight-backed pew which the Sawyer family had rented for five generations. The kerosene lamps in the chandelier above the worshipers cast a warm glow across the sanctuary, and the sputtering lamp on its pedestal beside the pulpit shone across Parson Baxter's face, giving him a radiance Rebecca thought to be heavenly as he warmed to his sermon topic, "God's Perfect Gift." Beeswax candles ensconced in princess pine wreaths on each windowsill completed the effect.

Few hymn books were raised as the worshipers rose to sing "Hark, the Herald Angels Sing," since the dim light of the ceiling lamps enabled only those directly beneath to make out the words and notes. Had it been a city church, gaslights would have brilliantly illuminated the room, but here, only kerosene and wax lent their glow over God's people. But never mind; the angelic light of the fields of Bethlehem that night caused the crowd to glow with true Christmas cheer. Most knew the words to Wesley's classic hymn anyway, so the singing was little hindered.

No happier crowd could be found anywhere on earth, thought Rebecca, as she joined the others in song. Never mind that off-key Uncle Jerry dominated one section of the church. Never mind that the old pump organ's bellows were so badly in need of leathers that it seemed to wheeze and gasp as Mrs. Baxter pumped it vigorously. A joyful noise unto the Lord was heard that evening as the Spirit of the Lord moved the spirit of the crowd, and the congregation raised its voice in glad unison.

The carols were sung, the Scripture was read, Reverend Baxter preached, and the benediction was offered in prayer. A caroling party to follow the Christmas Eve service was already forming in the vestry at the rear of the meetinghouse. Pairs, rather than a group, Rebecca noticed, seemed to be the order of the evening. Quite willing to have linked arms with Emma Jane Perkins, or even with one of her own brothers, Rebecca hesitated at the door when she noticed that Emma Jane was in the glad possession of Abijah Flagg, and Mark, as she had expected, was doing his manly best to impress Thirza.

Jenny and Fanny had formed a twosome, Rebecca noticed. But Brother John would no doubt keep her company, so she began to thread her way through the crowd of young people to where he stood warming himself at the vestry stove.

But by the time Rebecca reached the stove, John was not to be seen. She caught a glimpse of him, looking awkwardly handsome in a too-tight jacket drawn over his wool sweater as he steered the belle of Riverboro, sixteen-year-old Persis Watson, the merchant's daughter, out the hall door. Persis, who had been a freshman at Wareham Academy during Rebecca's senior year, had been the only girl on campus from a small village who could truly compete with Portland's Munjoy Hill crowd. Yet, unlike Huldah, Persis was not one to flaunt her dress. Always in good taste, her clothes, purchased in an annual shopping trip to Boston, were fine and well-fitting without ostentation.

Never had Rebecca felt more alone, yet in a crowd. Her brothers were occupied with romantic interests; Emma was taken. Younger children, who often flocked around

Rebecca for comfort and sisterly solace, were gone with their parents, for this was an almost-grown-up affair.

A touch on her elbow, and a voice spoke in her ear, "The stars are out—why don't we go out?" Like the battery-operated electric light display Rebecca had once seen lighting a store in Portland, she came to life. It was Adam Ladd!

"Mr. Aladdin, I didn't see *you* in the service!"

"That's nothing to wonder at. I came in late and sat upstairs."

"Horse lose a shoe?" Rebecca chirped.

"No horseshoes—no horse, either," Adam answered pleasantly. "I walked over from Aunt Mary's in North Riverboro. But who needs a horse for caroling? Let's get going."

"Gladly. But I have to be sure Mother and Aunt Jane are getting home all right. My brothers have hitched that frisky stallion to Grandpa Sawyer's old sleigh, and I'm not certain either Mother or Aunt Jane can manage him. John and Mark seem too occupied to take them home."

"*You're* the expert horsewoman, I take it," Adam chuckled.

"I *have* driven Dick-Boy a couple of times. I drove him here, and I guess I can drive him back! At least he stops when I tell him to."

"Who wouldn't?" Adam quipped. "Creatures with more sense than horses have been moved by your voice—or should I say, less sense?"

They now stood beside the horse-and-sleigh rigs in which Aunt Jane and the Randalls had arrived. "I'll drive you home first, Mother," John was telling Aurelia Randall as Rebecca and Adam approached.

"Why don't you an' Jane ride home with me 'n Jerry?" interrupted Aunt Sarah Cobb. "Then John kin have his horse an' sleigh for the evening."

"Shore," agreed Uncle Jerry. "We'll git you wimmen home."

"But that won't work, either," John protested in exasperation, yet reluctant to explain.

"But why?" Mother was clearly puzzled. Rebecca, however, noticed that Persis was watching the carolers trickle off in a long, thin line down the road in the light of the moon. She appeared dismayed at this turn of events. Persis clearly was not the forward type, and though she could enjoy John's companionship, she obviously did not want him to herself alone on their first date.

"May I speak?" Rebecca stopped the entire discussion with her firm, incisive query. "I think Mr. Ladd and I can help out, if you'll let us," she suggested. "I'm sure Mr. Ladd and I can manage Dick-Boy if you and Aunt Jane want to ride home with the Cobbs," Rebecca remarked. John grinned slyly, and he and Persis were moving after the carolers before Rebecca finished talking.

"I'll go along with that," Adam pleasantly put in. He offered Aurelia his arm for a boost into the two-seater, then passed her cane and drew the buffalo robe back as Aunt Jane clambered in from the other side.

"Why were you afoot tonight?" Rebecca asked as she and Adam rode toward the carolers, who could be heard singing, "O Little Town of Bethlehem" for old Widow Trask, who lived alone in a neat little shingled cottage at a bend where the Acreville Road joins Riverboro's one street.

"Actually, I don't own a horse," Adam explained. "I'm sure you know that when I visit Aunt Mary for the holidays I usually rent a team at the livery stable near the depot in Maplewood. But the stable had rented out its last horse and locked up for the night by the time the train got in from Portland this afternoon. The stagecoach had already left for Riverboro, but I did manage to hitch a ride with Hillard Robinson, who'd gone to the depot to pick up a new bean winnower he'd ordered. You can't believe how long it takes to walk a team of workhorses from Maplewood!"

"You were lucky to be here at all!"

"I'll say! I barely had time to swallow a plate of Aunt Mary's baked beans and head out the door. I had to sit in the balcony, and by the time I got downstairs after the benediction, you were out of sight. I thought I'd have to walk home alone."

Adam tied Dick-Boy to the stump of a wind-blasted, gnarled maple tree as Rebecca, who for once restrained herself, waited demurely for him to hand her down from the sleigh. They joined the others in a couple more carols, sung lustily until the old widow opened her door. "Won't ye come in," Mrs. Trask asked, her voice cracking as she tried to make herself heard. "I've got some hot mulled ciduh an' doughnuts."

"We can't let those kids go in there," Adam protested. "They'll eat up that poor woman's entire winter supply of food."

Rebecca giggled. "Oh, come on. I know her better'n that. She has so much cider pressed each fall from the Wolf Rivers apples in her orchard that she supplies the whole town with vinegar every spring. As for doughnuts, she's about worn out her kitchen windowsill passing them out to every kid that comes by. Likely she's been frying doughnuts for days so she can feed us tonight."

Inside, the crowd stood shoulder to shoulder, munching home-made doughnuts and gulping mugs of hot cider spiced with cinnamon and cloves. Thirza Meserve singed a hole in a silk stocking when a red spark jumped through the stove grate where she had gone to get warm, complaining of the draft by the door. "Ouch!" cried Thirza, and she added in a hoarse whisper, "Someone should tell Mrs. Trask not to put pitch-pine knots in the stove when she's expecting company."

"Sh-h-h!" replied Mark, embarrassed.

"You take me home this instant, Mark Randall."

Mark obliged and preceded Thirza out the door. "Huldah will *never* forgive me for ruining her best hose," Thirza was heard to remark as she stepped outside.

"If Huldah ever finds out how they got a hole in them, she might not, indeed," Rebecca said quietly to Adam.

"There's something strangely familiar about that young lady who left so suddenly with your brother, Mark, tonight," Adam remarked later as Dick-Boy kept up a steady trot along River Road, which connects Acreville Road to Maplewood Road, then mounts the hills into North Riverboro. "I had the uncomfortable feeling that someone very like her had tried to get my attention a few years ago."

"And no wonder," Rebecca added, amused. "Thirza's sister Huldah was a student at Wareham; she graduated a year ahead of me."

"Oh, ho—the coy one who thought Wareham boys too young for her tastes."

"The same," Rebecca replied, sobered now as she considered that Thirza, young as she was, was interested in Mark. "Kids grow up too fast," she said at last.

"And we grow old," Adam put in, turning Rebecca's comment to his own purposes. Horse and sleigh crested a grade and with a "Whoa, Dick-Boy," he drew the great dapple-gray animal to a halt. Far, far to the north, long gold fingers curtained in a vast lavender and pink veil convoluted and flashed in the northern sky as Adam and Rebecca sat for a time in silent awe.

"Oh!" Rebecca exclaimed, patting Adam's arm with one gloved hand as she pointed to an unusually long flash with the other. "What do you suppose the northern lights really are?"

"*Aurora borealis,* named after the sun god of the Greeks," Adam commented with a chuckle. "How little we know about a phenomenon, when we think we know so much. We give something a fancy name tied to ancient times, and we humans presumptuously imagine we understand it."

"But what *are* they?" Rebecca insisted.

"Possibly electrical energy; perhaps solar energy from the sun. As with many phenomena, we give it a nice, scientific label, then we smugly assume we've explained it," he said. "We seem to like playing God, almost."

"Like names?" Rebecca asked, teasing.

"How do you mean?"

"People seem so mysterious until we learn their names. Then we think all of a sudden we know all about them," Rebecca replied. "Later, when their character begins to show through, we learn how wrong we were."

"Will I ever know *you,* I wonder," Adam answered merrily. With a cluck to Dick-Boy he sent horse and sleigh in motion. "We'd best be getting on. If you don't mind, I'd like to drive over to Aunt Mary's, so she won't worry. You'd better phone your mother from there."

"You're right!" Rebecca agreed. "And I shouldn't stay too late. It's my first Christmas with my family since I left Sunnybrook Farm as a little girl, you know."

Adam did not answer right away. The jingle of the sleigh bells, the "chuck-chuck-chuck-chuck" of Dick-Boy's hooves muffled in the snow, the rumble of runners as they hit a bare patch of road gravel now and then, the soughing and sighing of the wind in the pines along the roadside—all else was silence. Then, as the yellow glow of the lamp in Aunt Mary's window came into view, Adam spoke. "If . . . if I had a family to go home to, how happy I could be," he said in a voice hoarse with emotion.

Rebecca could not answer his plaint; instead she wrapped the fingers of both hands around his arm and buried her face in the sleeve of his cashmere overcoat.

The evening with Adam ended much sooner than Rebecca would have liked, certainly. After a supper of hot tomato soup and toast at Aunt Mary Ladd's, and a nose bag of oats for Dick-Boy, Adam drove her back to the brick house. "I promised you your daughter back by eight o'clock, and here she is," Adam quipped to Aurelia, as he brought Rebecca to the door.

"I'll put the team in the barn now," Mark offered, pushing past his mother at the sight of Dick-Boy and the sleigh drawn up in the circle drive.

"You'll do nothing of the sort until you've driven Mr. Ladd back to North Riverboro," Aurelia admonished him. "And don't say, 'Can't John do it?' John's not back from Watson's yet."

Adam only chuckled as he turned to leave. He squeezed Rebecca's hand, then walked to the sleigh to wait while Mark put on his mackinaw and stocking cap.

11

A CHRISTMAS TO REMEMBER

Christmas Day did not come at the brick house as early as Rebecca had remembered its arrival at Sunnybrook Farm, since there was no herd of cows waiting to be milked at five in the morning. The only livestock besides the cat and her five kittens was the chickens, Dick-Boy, and the old jersey cow, all of whom would wait happily until daybreak for breakfast. Molly was a once-a-day cow, making her an ideal family milk producer, since it made little difference to her whether she was milked at eight o'clock or ten—she'd always give her five quarts of milk, with cream enough for butter.

There had been some heated discussion late Christmas Eve whether Santa Claus really would arrive at the brick house. The gifts were already under the tree, though the only one at all resembling a toy was a varnished Flexible Flyer sled with real steel runners which Rebecca had bought for Fanny, though she felt guilty for weeks for having dipped into her share of the Sunnybrook settlement to purchase anything so extravagant.

At Sunnybrook in Rebecca's childhood, seven woolen stockings had hung on nails under the sitting room mantel each Christmas Eve; and each Christmas morning the Randall children had found them filled with whatever modest pleasures Saint Nicholas had deemed worthy for so humble a household. But at the brick house, though indeed there were mantelpieces in every room, the fireplaces under them had long since been plastered over. Only a six-inch stovepipe protruding from each black-iron stove into the wall now remained as an entrance for the round, jolly old elf. All agreed that only a very addled Santa would dare enter through such an ignoble passage as a metal flue—all, that is, except Rebecca and Fanny, who was about the age Rebecca had been when last she had enjoyed Christmas with her family at Sunnybrook.

So, from the mothballs in her dresser, Aunt Jane produced a pair of knee-length woolen socks. "I knitted these for Father just before he died, but he never got to wear them," Aunt Jane explained. "I couldn't bear to give them away. So I guess we kin put 'em t' good use t'night, fer the two who still believe in Santa. Aurelia, you can be the jolly fat man," she added, smiling primly through misty eyes.

❧ ❧ ❧

The dawn had not yet begun to redden the crest of Guide Board Hill when Rebecca was wakened by someone in her room. "Becky—you awake?"

"Fanny, go back to bed. It's not a school morning. We were up late last night."

"Let's check our stockings."

Rebecca struck a match. Five-fifteen, read her alarm clock, and she had set it to ring at seven. "Crawl in with me. We'll go downstairs at six."

"Promise?"

"I promise."

For the seventeenth time, at least, Fanny's sharp heels had dug into Rebecca's ribs. Thc pads on a child's heels turn to solid bone at bedtime, Rebecca had learned from times when she had shared her bed before, and now she tossed and turned, unable to go back to sleep. Finally, giving up trying to catch the sandman again, she sat up, struck a match, and lit her favorite lamp—a small one on a blue willow base with a handle given her by Adam one Christmas after she and Emma Jane had sold him the soap. Though it was still only a quarter to six, Rebecca grabbed her pillow and shoved a blanket in Fanny's arms. Silently big sister and little crept downstairs and into the parlor.

Rebecca paid little attention to the small gifts and goodies Santa Claus—Aurelia—had hastily crammed into the socks. Each girl found a candy cane, a neatly folded linen handkerchief, red delicious apples wrapped in tissue, a handful of walnuts, and far down in the toe, a Florida orange apiece, a costly, once-a-winter treat from the land of sunshine.

Fanny took the lamp and scurried into the kitchen and returned with a paring knife as Rebecca shook the ashes out of the parlor stove's grate and placed splinters of old split cedar rails over the coals until they burst into flame. Then, chucking in a couple of junks of rock maple, she shut the stove and watched in contentment as Fanny peeled her orange. Rebecca was soon conscious that she, herself, was glowing as warmly as the stove behind her. Fanny's delight with the Christmas stocking and the gift of the orange, Rebecca felt, could only have been excelled by the delight of the Mother Mary at the gifts of the Magi.

When Mother and Aunt Jane came into the parlor at seven o'clock, the first rays of a rosy December dawn had begun to illuminate the tinsel and crystal ornaments on the tall balsam. But, rolled together in an old comforter, Rebecca and Fanny slept happily beside the stove.

After a breakfast of hasty pudding with milk and molasses, coffee, and oranges (neither Rebecca nor Fanny felt slighted that they had eaten their oranges early), the seven family members—five children, Mother, and Aunt Jane—trooped into the parlor. Mother quickly designated Jenny and Fanny to hand out the gifts, but then she asked them all to wait quietly while John read the Christmas story. He had come prepared with his small, battered leather-bound old Bible.

"John," asked Rebecca, "as the hostess of the brick house, do I get to choose the Bible?"

"Well, I guess so, Becky."

She stepped under the arch into the sitting room. From the writing table drawer she pulled out a heavy reference Bible, bound in limp black leather, its gilt edges mellowed to a barely discernible yellow. Stamped in still-legible gold letters on the cover was DEA. ISRAEL SAWYER.

"Why," cried Mother, "it's Father's Bible—your grandfather's! I haven't seen it since *my* last Christmas here—just before Lorenzo and I were married!"

Rebecca and Aurelia embraced. Both were crying. "You've come home, Mother," Rebecca choked. "And *I've* come home, too." The parlor was quiet as Mother returned to the platform rocker that had been Aunt Miranda's and before that Grandmother Sawyer's. Rebecca passed John the Bible, and he stood before the Christmas tree with the rays of the morning sun filtering through it from the east window and illuminating the pages.

"John, your grandfather would have read about the visit of the Magi, from Matthew chapter two," Aunt Jane prompted him.

John read verses one through eleven, concluding with thesc words:

> And when they were come into the house, they saw the young child with Mary his mother, and fell down, and worshipped him: and when they had opened their treasures, they presented unto him gifts; gold, and frankincense, and myrrh.

John then prayed, thanking the Lord for the greatest gift, His Son, and for "the gift of God, which is that eternal life which we may have by faith in Him who died for us. In Jesus' name, amen."

The joy Rebecca felt that morning as the gifts were opened knew no bounds. Magnificent as was their tree, the gifts that Christmas were frugal for the most part. Though blessed with modest wealth from the sale of Sunnybrook, Aurelia and her children were wise enough to realize that the money must be invested against future living expenses and academy and college tuitions, rather than squandered.

So the gifts were simple and there were few surprises: knit socks from Aunt Jane for both boys; knit mittens for Rebecca and her sisters. Aprons, corduroy pants, crocheted doilies, several books, a new Bible for John; and a pair of fine leather boots for Mother from Mark and John who had pooled their resources to purchase them by mail order. Aurelia hadn't needed shoes last winter, since abed, then a wheelchair had been her lot. Now she got around pretty well with a cane, and more and more she left it in the hall umbrella stand for outdoor excursions only. Except that there were no longer any toys under the Randall tree, Rebecca noticed, things had changed little since her childhood.

Rebecca, alone, splurged, and her single indulgence was the steel-frame sled for Fanny—a five-foot-long Flexible Flyer, "the biggest one made," Mr. Watson, the storekeeper, had told her confidently. He had had it since last year; and when in two seasons he had not sold it for seven dollars, he had marked it down to five, "just to get my money back."

Rebecca had passed that sled at the store's entrance every time she shopped at Watson's Mercantile for some weeks. Tugging at her heart was the fact that she, Rebecca, had never had a sled. And now Fanny, at twelve, was just a bit older than Rebecca when she had left Sunnybrook. Then, too, there was the unfinished, handmade sled Mark had discovered in the Sunnybrook barn's rafters just before the auction. Their father had begun it, and under his skilled hands it promised to become a masterpiece. But Lorenzo Randall had been stricken with pneumonia, and his music had been left unplayed, his sled unmade.

How Rebecca's heart had ached the day Mark found that forgotten sled. She had seen it once, when as a small girl she and big sister Hannah had been clambering across the rafters pretending to be raiding Indians.

That sled was sold in the auction, but the old story Mother had told—of Father coughing and spitting as he worked with his drawknife and block plane on the seasoned maple boards to finish the sled long ago, of his taking to his bed, from which he never arose—this tale haunted Rebecca each time she passed the new sled in Watson's store. Fanny, Rebecca knew, would by another year disdain sleds as she already did dolls. The die was cast, her purse was opened, and Rebecca bought the sled.

The sled was not long a secret at the brick house, however, for it appeared under the Christmas tree tagged with Fanny's name the very evening the tree was set up in the parlor. So Mark had for several days made preparation for a grand sledding party on the slopes behind the barn.

The flat meadows of the Saco River's intervale were thickly crusted with ice from a mid-December sleet storm following a heavy snowfall. Mark worked on the slopes with a shovel until the uneven places were smoothed for a downhill run which would gain momentum to carry sled and passengers across the fields. He enlisted Jenny and Fanny to help him tote buckets of water on successive evenings and these were splashed liberally across spots he had smoothed with his shovel, freezing solid and making a wild sled run indeed.

So Fanny, toting her prized Flexible Flyer, followed Mark through the shed and barn and out the barnyard door that Christmas morning as soon as they had pulled on leggings, wool socks, and oiled leather boots. Rebecca, Jenny, and John trailed behind, while Mother and Aunt Jane waited at the kitchen window.

Fanny lost her nerve at the top of the steep grade, and she sent Mark down first—which was exactly what he had secretly hoped for. Everyone but John took turns at the brief but wild ride, terminating in a snowdrift next to a clump of currant bushes.

"Okay," Mark announced, when Fanny's turn came round again, "take 'er 'cross the meadow, Sis. I figguh if you aim fer that big ol' pine down by the swimmin' hole, you kin git most of the way across—nearly a mile."

"That's a long way to walk back," Fanny protested. "I want you to come with me."

"All right," Mark willingly agreed. He stretched himself full length on the sled and invited Fanny to climb on top. "Hug me tight," he cried. Rebecca gave them a shove, and they were off.

Far, far across the fields the sled glided. At last, when her brother and sister were just a speck in the distance, Rebecca saw that Mark had steered the Flyer toward the river, then down the embankment out of sight. She was unconcerned at first; she knew that the river was frozen solid. "That rascal," she told John and Jenny. "Mark's going to have to carry Fanny. She'll be tuckered out before she's halfway home."

John went inside the barn to feed Dick-Boy, and Jenny, heeding Molly's insistent lowing, decided it was time to coax her to let down her milk and gather the eggs. Rebecca waited by herself for Mark and Fanny to reappear above the river bank. Long moments passed, and she began to worry. Inwardly she began to chasten herself for having bought the sled. "It was an extravagance," she said, imagining a pool of open water, or perhaps a log or stone under the riverbank, where her brother and sister lay unconscious.

Determined at last to see what was the matter, Rebecca made her way down the slope. She trod across the icy field, and she was already a good distance from the barn when she heard Jenny's excited shouts behind her.

"Mark and Fanny, they're . . ." Rebecca heard her yell; the rest of the sentence was lost in the breeze.

"I'm going after them," Rebecca called back, and she continued her determined journey.

Jenny continued to shout, but Rebecca kept on walking. Finally, "Becky, come back here" came through clearly as the breeze shifted. Reluctantly, she heeded Jenny's call and returned to the barn. "Mark and Fanny are at Robinson's," snapped a very exasperated Jenny. "They just phoned to say they are walking home by the road, since it's better footing than across the field."

By the time Mark and Fanny had plodded home—Mark pulling Fanny on the sled more than halfway—the ladies had dinner ready. This year's bird was a spring goose, purchased just a week earlier from Hillard Robinson. At Sunnybrook the Christmas bird had always been a rooster, not as large as a turkey to be sure, but ample and juicy all the same.

But John had read that the traditional Christmas bird in merrie olde England was goose. Though waterfowl were birds of quite a different feather for the Randalls and Sawyers, and the bird of tradition at the brick house had for years been turkey, Mother and Aunt Jane took it in good sport when John brought home a full-grown, fat Toulouse gander from Robinson's. But the goose refused to submit to the chopping block, so John had to dispatch it with his twelve-gauge shotgun, which so upset Aunt Jane that she said at first she couldn't bear to eat any.

But the aroma of baking goose in a wood-fired oven will tame the queasiest stomach. Jane soon found that the goose supplied far more drippings for gravy than either turkey or chicken. So she put behind her memories of its violent demise as she helped prepare bowls of boiled potatoes and onions, mashed buttercup squash, and plum pudding and mince pies for dessert.

Jenny joined Fanny and Mark in the afternoon for several more sled runs across the meadows, down the river, where it bent around Guide Board Hill with the Robinson farmstead atop, and at last gliding to a stop by the plank bridge on Acreville Road. These coasting trips, during which the girls took turns riding with Mark, took nearly an hour each, so the three younger children kept themselves occupied for the entire afternoon. During his return from the second of these trips, Mark met John driving Dick-Boy and giving Persis Watson a sleigh ride. But Mark did not envy his brother's happy situation, having had enough of romance the evening before to last him a long, long time.

Rebecca, though she was savoring thoroughly her Christmas with her family, found her heart beating just a bit faster when the phone rang and Aunt Jane announced, "It's for you, Becky." The first call was from Emma Jane, graciously announcing that Abijah was there "with Squire Bean's double sleigh an' span of drivin' hosses," and "would you like to join us for a drive in about an hour?"

Rebecca, not one to sit and wait for the phone to ring, agreed at once. But the phone did ring as soon as she hung up the receiver. It was Adam. "May I visit you for a few moments? I'd like to bring over some trinkets for you and your family."

"But you have no horse," Rebecca protested.

"I've borrowed an old nag from across the road. Aunt Mary has an old cutter in her stable. It's not much of a rig, to be sure, but it'll get me there."

Rebecca agreed at once, on the condition that Adam join her with Emma and Abijah in a sleigh ride. It was settled, and an hour later Adam arrived just in time to put his borrowed steed in the empty stall next to Dick-Boy's before Abijah and Emma arrived.

It was a glorious winter afternoon, though the sun hung low in the southern sky and the chill of the northern New England air bit through even the sturdy buffalo robes in Squire Bean's sleigh. But the seats were narrow, so Rebecca and Emma Jane found they had no trouble keeping warm, as neither Abijah nor Adam seemed to mind the girls' sitting close enough for comfort.

Down lanes thickly overhung with snowy hemlocks they drove, across wooden bridges, then along stone walls, where squirrels followed on cedar rails running atop the walls, keeping pace with the horses' trotting hooves. At last, toward dusk, Abijah swung the horses around Guide Board Hill and onto Riverboro's one street just in time to overtake Mark dragging Fanny on her new Flyer toward home. Abijah held the horses while Mark hitched the sled rope on behind, and the six of them had a merry ride indeed for the last mile back to the brick house.

As Adam walked toward the barn to get his borrowed horse, Abijah stopped him. "You've got a broken runner on that sleigh, Adam," he said, pointing to Aunt Mary's ancient cutter sitting by the barn's double doors. "You won't get a mile with it."

Adam bent to look closer, and Rebecca and Emma Jane joined the examination of the old conveyance. "Worn out, for sure," Emma Jane piped up. "An' the other one's nearly worn through, too."

"Tongue-tied Miss Perkins, who couldn't sell soap to a stranger," responded Adam, surprised.

Emma Jane reddened. "My pa's a blacksmith an' a farrier, and his shop is just across the bridge. He's teachin' me the business end of smithin' so's he can tend to work. He says a woman needs to know business—not all are fortunate enough to marry a man who can manage money," Emma defended herself.

"That she does!" Adam agreed. "Fortunate indeed is the man who marries a woman who can not only balance his books, but who can appraise his stock in trade," he chuckled. "But, say I leave Aunt Mary's sleigh here for your dad to fix? How much for two new steel runners, and when will it be ready?"

"Five dollars apiece; be ready by five tomorrow," Emma Jane answered with a confidence developed from dealing with her father's customers in the months since she had left Wareham Academy.

"I'm heading back to Boston on the morning train. Can you deliver it to North Riverboro?"

"Sure. Delivery's a dollar more."

Adam produced a gold eagle and a silver dollar. "Eleven dollars in advance, and I'll expect good workmanship," he said with a chuckle, passing her the money. And turning to Rebecca he added, "I guess I'm going to have to borrow a saddle to ride my horse back to its owner."

"No need," Abijah interrupted. "We'll take you home when you're ready. Your horse'll trot right along behind on a rope."

The stars were out as Abijah, Emma, and Rebecca drove back from North Riverboro. As they topped the hill from where Rebecca and Adam had viewed the spectacular northern lights the night before, Rebecca could see the yellow gleam of lamps in the windows of Riverboro on the frozen Saco far below. *I'm all alone again,* she thought, *alone in my own little harbor.* Adam would leave for Boston before dawn, she knew. But for Rebecca, he was already gone. *Is this real?* she asked herself. *Will it ever be real, or am I playing at romance, like Mark last evening with Thirza?*

In the seat in front of her Rebecca could see the silhouettes of two heads—the manly one in bowler and ear muffs, the other, ringed with curls and done up in rabbit fur, laid against the young man's shoulder. As she smiled and closed her eyes, Rebecca's dreams seemed to repeat themselves with the steady beat of the horses' hooves. And her dreams were sweet indeed.

12

THE LETTER FROM PORTLAND

The day after New Year's found Rebecca and Emma Jane skating on the millpond ice above the dam. Arm in arm they circled, etching parallel patterns, like giant scrollwork, far out on the glassy surface, further even than the lovers who had wandered on skates for hours two nights earlier in the flickering light of a bonfire of burning Christmas trees.

It was one of those rare days before the heavy snows blanket the ponds and lakes of New England until April, when skating can be enjoyed without shoveling and scraping. The thermometer had risen above freezing for a day and a night in the week following Christmas, and several hours' warm rain had melted the snow and put a sheet of water on the already substantial ice of the pond. Now it had frozen hard, making a seamless surface from shore to shore. Today, though, it was snowing, with flakes as big as pine shavings, and so the girls decided to have one last skate while the pond ice was still clear.

The youngest Randalls were in school that day, and just at daybreak, John had buttoned on his mackinaw and trudged off to Squire Bean's. Emma had ridden the stage-coach to Maplewood and back New Year's Day to see Abijah off to college on the Brunswick train. She had slept on the hard seat most of the way back to Riverboro, and Abijah had slept on his journey to Bowdoin, as well—New Year's Eve skating parties can be very tiring indeed!

Rebecca had heard from Adam Ladd once since Christmas. He had written a short letter thanking her for a good time Christmas Day. "I must visit Maine at least once a month, even in winter," Adam had written, "for Aunt Mary is growing old, and it is important that I look in on her occasionally and see to her welfare." As a post-script he added, "Please write me often, for it gets very lonely here in Boston during the winter."

Except for a Valentine card the previous winter, Rebecca recalled, this was the first note which he had not written on his business stationery. He had signed it, "With Fondest Regards, Adam." Rebecca took special notice, too, that for the first time he had not signed his full name.

"Remember when we first skated like this—you with your Aunt Jane's old skates with socks stuffed in the toes!" Emma giggled as, backs to the breeze, they sailed toward the old sawmill on the far side.

"Seven winters ago," Rebecca affirmed thoughtfully. "That makes a week of winters. I wonder if there's any significance in that?"

"Always philosophizing! You haven't changed a bit," said Emma Jane in mock disgust. "We've grown older and learned to love each other during seven years, that's all. It might have been six years or eight, or five or nine."

"I guess you're right. But things have changed. You have a beau—and who'd have thought I'd be the mistress of the brick house."

"You can have your big ol' brick house. I'm having a little cottage for two!"

"Is there something you're not telling me, Miss Rich Blacksmith's daughter? Did Abijah . . . !"

"Yes, he did—New Year's Eve when we were skating on this very pond! And I said yes, I'd marry him, and he's bringing me a diamond ring when he comes home in March for spring vacation, and we're getting married in June, and I'm asking you right now to be my maid of honor."

"What did your parents say? I can guess—your dad said to wait a year, and your mother said to get married next weekend," Rebecca merrily chortled. She was now skating backwards to watch Emma's animated face as they talked. They had turned around into the wind, going back toward the Perkins's blacksmith shop, with Emma pushing against Rebecca.

"I haven't told them yet. I'm waiting for the ring. I . . . "

At this juncture, Rebecca, who had been holding both Emma's gloved hands in her own, interrupted with a shriek. "What is *that* galloping across the ice?" She let go of one of Emma's hands and pointed in surprise at a long-haired creature bouncing gaily toward them from the far side of the millpond.

Emma pirouetted on her skates and whirled around beside Rebecca.

"Is that Jehu?" Rebecca continued in agitated surprise.

"The same noble beast," Emma laughed. Both girls again pirouetted, to skate side by side.

"But I saw that old buck sheep of your father's just on the edge of the ice last week trying his desperate best to get back on high ground. Surely he wouldn't venture that far out—and he's skipping like a lamb in clover!"

A merry, wicked glint of glee shone in Emma Jane's blue eyes at the consternation on the face of her dark-eyed friend.

"Remember that my mother phoned yours to ask that she speak to Mark about him and some other boys snow-balling Jehu, Father's ram?"

"Yes." Rebecca was embarrassed, puzzled.

"What Mother didn't know was, she needn't have made the phone call."

"How so?" Rebecca arched one raven eyebrow.

"Papa had tied Jehu to his anvil the night before after work an' fixed him up with a set of small, steel ox shoes, two on each hoof. When the boys chased him onto the ice with snowballs the next day, he turned on 'em and ran them off the ice. Now Jehu roams all over the millpond like it was his own domain. Did you ask Mark how he got his britches torn?"

"That scamp! He tricked me into patching the leg of his corduroy pants! You mean? That's why he didn't ask Mother to sew them up!"

"Papa said it was the funniest thing he'd ever seen," Emma Jane giggled. "He said if he hadn't chased Jehu off with a stick, he might have damaged more than just Mark's pants."

For one of the few times in her life, Rebecca was speechless. Finally Emma interrupted her indignant ruminations. "You've never told me about your trip to Brunswick or your interview at Deering Oaks. How'd it turn out?"

"I'm not going," Rebecca said evenly, adding, "I don't believe the Lord wants me there." She went on, telling Emma Jane about Mrs. Stowe's advice and of her decision at the Maplewood post office.

"*I'd* have snapped up an offer like that in a minute," Emma Jane responded confidently. "Mebbe their kids *are* all spoiled rotten, like you say. But think of the advantages—money, a free college education—you could be a missionary, like you used to talk about, after you got some money in the bank."

"A man's life consisteth not in the abundance of things which he possesseth," Rebecca quoted Jesus quietly. "I suppose I must sound pious, and now that I *own* the brick house and my family has a little money, I may even seem hypocritical. I wanted money once, but it was to pay Mother's mortgage. Now that the mortgage is paid, I'm truly grateful, and I want to spend my life doing things that count for eternity." Then as an afterthought she added with a laugh, "I'd like a new hat now and then of course."

"But what do you want to *do?*" Emma Jane was perplexed to think that anyone could want more than she and Rebecca both now had—good homes, families that loved them, money to satisfy their needs, if not their greeds.

"Oh, if my life were as simple as Jehu's," she cried in mock melancholy as the old Merino sheep bounded past. "New shoes and he's king of the ice—free and not a care."

"It'd be a dull life, I'm afraid," shot back Emma.

"There you go, talking like me at last," said Rebecca. "But to tell the truth, I'm not sure what I want to do," she said hesitantly. "I did get a letter from the Maine Home for Little Wayfarers just before Christmas. Aunt Jane says it's an orphanage in Portland which helps the orphans of immigrants who died of disease and left no money to send their children back to their families in Europe."

❧ ❧ ❧

That evening, alone in her room, Rebecca lit the lamp on her bedside commode and pulled open its single drawer. From it she drew a long, thin white envelope, which contained a neatly penned business letter.

Dear Miss Randall,

Your name has been given us as a candidate for the position of housemother. Your responsibilities would require twenty-four-hour on-call duty, with one day, Saturday evening to Sunday evening, free every two weeks. You would be responsible for supervising about thirty girls, ages seven to fourteen, during the early morning and evening hours when they are not in school, as well as supervising their play on Saturday and accompanying them to church every other week. You would, of course, be expected to be available to nurse them when they were ill and unable to attend school, and to be on call during night hours if a child in your dormitory were ill or needed attention.

Since ours is an organization of love and mercy to children, supported by the freewill offerings of God's people, our salary offer is necessarily modest: Five dollars a week, plus room (in dorm, shared bath), board, and laundry service.

We must have a commitment for this position by March, so your decision to come for an interview will be needed by January 31st. Please respond within thirty days, and we shall send round-trip train tickets by return mail.

The letter was signed by Miss Edythe Leonard, headmistress, Maine Home for Little Wayfarers, Munjoy Hill, Portland. Rebecca noticed that the members of the home's Council of Reference included Mr. Jacob J. Heywood, Boston and Down East Railway Co. Mr. Gould's signature, she recalled with great interest, had been on the contract for the sale of Sunnybrook Farm.

Crossing the room from her bed where she had been seated, Rebecca moved to her writing table by the window. The only piece of furniture Rebecca had kept for herself from the Sunnybrook auction, the handmade table with bookshelves at either end, had been her father's—he had made it, and its carefully joined planks of planed and hand-sanded maple showed the skill of a craftsman ncarly as talented with the joiner's tools as with the violin bow and harpsichord keys. If only Lorenzo Randall had had a larger market for his talents, his family might not have waited so long for their rewards.

Rebecca lighted the table lamp by her window. She now pulled her robe closer around her against the January chill which permeated the bricks and plaster of the old house. Her only source of heat was what weak warmth rose through her register from the kitchen stove below, whose cooking fire had long ago died out.

Rebecca drew a fresh sheet of linen paper from her stationery box, checked the nib on a hand-sharpened goose quill pen from the drawer, and flipped open the pewter lid of the grinning, fat-bellied imp with glass innards, which she had found in a Portland curio store. Then she dipped her pen into the ink and wrote:

> Dear Miss Leonard,
>
> I do gladly accept your invitation to come to Portland for an interview. Since at the present I [Here she paused, hesitant to write "am unemployed." Busy people are always the first ones asked to take on new responsibilities, she knew.] am not otherwise engaged, I am at your disposal to travel there at your earliest convenience.
>
> Cordially,
> Rebecca R. Randall

Though brother John, who would begin college in September, offered to accompany Rebecca to Portland, she insisted on traveling alone. "This is *my* trip," she said decidedly, but with laughter in her voice. Remembering how Emily Maxwell had guided her through the difficulties of the Brunswick journey a month earlier, she added quietly, "I want to give God a chance to direct my steps alone this time."

The reply from Miss Leonard came just a week later, and with it, a round-trip ticket from the Maplewood train station to Portland. Rebecca would have preferred to have taken the train from Riverboro's siding into Wareham so that she could have left a day early and put up with Miss Maxwell before proceeding on her journey. But Edythe Leonard, the careful manager of her institution's money, deemed the direct route—by stagecoach to Maplewood, then on to Portland without changing cars—to be the more frugal choice. The Lord had taken Rebecca at her word when she said she had determined to go alone.

"My soul, wait thou only upon God; for my expectation is from him," Rebecca read from Psalm 62:5 the evening before her departure. Carefully, with a blotted pen, she underscored the word *only* in her Bible.

❧ ❧ ❧

Three days later a beaming Rebecca bounced out of the stagecoach in the brick house's drive even before the driver could stop his horses. Leaving the coachman to bring her valise to the door stoop, she raced up the steps and into the front hall before Mother and Aunt Jane could even wash their hands from cutting up vegetables for a kettle of soup.

"Mother, Aunt Jane," she called with such unrestrained joy that her mother and aunt thought Rebecca had reverted to her childhood. She waved a sheaf of papers, then thrust them into Aurelia's hands. "I'm to begin August fifteen, and the children are the loveliest, most precious darlings you ever saw." Rebecca's childish glee at her triumph sobered as she added, "And, oh, some of them have such sad eyes – especially the new ones."

"What kind of a place is it?" Aurelia asked, catching Rebecca's enthusiasm.

"It's a home for children from all over New England who've lost both parents, especially children whose parents were from Europe. When their parents died they were left, in most cases, without a relative in America," she explained. "Some of these youngsters speak little English when they come. Such a lot of frightened little waifs you have never seen," she said. "I spent the first evening there rocking and singing to sleep Anna and Amanda, twin girls who had come there from Fall River, Massachusetts. Their parents brought them from Poland two years ago when they were only five. Their mom and dad, who had worked in a woolen mill, both died of tuberculosis right after Christmas. Such a sight of needy children you never saw!"

"If the need is so great, why don't they want you 'til the middle of August?" inquired Aunt Jane through her tears. "If I were younger, I'd go myself right now."

"How you talk, Jane," put in Aurelia. "You're the one who thought Rebecca should wait until spring before travelin'."

"I thought 'twas foolish for her to travel t' Brunswick jest t' hear a speech," she defended, "but when there's people that need you, I say, 'Go!'"

"They've got all the help they need right now, Auntie," Rebecca explained. "Their present girls' housemother's getting married in June, and I'm to take her place."

"But you don't begin 'til August," Aurelia protested. "With the children out of school, won't they need help in the summer?"

"Actually, most of my work with the children won't begin until after Labor Day," explained Rebecca. "I'm going there two weeks early to help get things ready for the fall."

"So what happens to the children in summer?" said Jane in exasperation.

"They farm 'em out," Rebecca answered nonchalantly.

"Farm out?" Aurelia inquired, dismayed.

"Oh!" said Jane, clearly concerned.

"Miss Leonard explained that the children are all sent to farms across the state for the summer. They are let out to farmers, where they pick berries or peas or help with the haying or tend the chickens all summer, in exchange for room and board. Most of the older ones stay on the farms through September, to help pick corn or pick up potatoes."

"Dear me," said Aunt Jane, "they do expect a lot from those children."

"Caring for orphans is expensive," Rebecca defended. "Besides *I* did garden work enough when I was small myself."

"Let's look at it this way," Aurelia said, "your work will be with the *children*. You're not responsible for the way they do things."

"Mother is right, of course," Rebecca told herself later. But Aurelia's reference to "the way they do things" troubled Rebecca, and she made herself a mental note that though she was going to the Home for Wayfarers to work with children, she'd take a good, hard look at how things ran there and see if she could change things for the better.

13

A VALENTINE TRAGEDY

Rebecca had received five letters from Adam Ladd in the six weeks since Christmas, and she had sent him seven replies. His first letter had been warm but brief, but since he had added that he sometimes got "very lonely," Rebecca determined to touch his loneliness by exposing a tiny mite of her own growing affection for her "Mr. Aladdin." She hoped that he would respond in kind. So it was now no longer a question of who wrote whom first; each letter was full of news, questions, and more importantly, the deepest thoughts of the soul tormented by near-love which insisted on being expressed to another soul suffering like torments.

Rebecca had felt guilty, though not for long, about her fourth letter to Adam. He had written her three letters, and she had sent him three in reply. The day after she had mailed him the third, it occurred to her, on rereading Adam's third letter, that she had not fully answered his query about whether a husband should take first place in his wife's life, or should Christ have that place. Much exercised that she put the Lord first, Rebecca had written that St. Paul had taught that an "unmarried woman careth for the things of the Lord," but that a married woman "careth . . . how she may please her husband." It was on Friday that she mailed that letter.

Then on Sunday Parson Baxter had preached on "The Wife as an Ensample of the Church," and he had pointed out that as husbands portray Christ, wives portray Christ's church, His holy Bride. In living a godly life with her husband, a Christian wife reaches her highest calling, for, said the good parson, "she thus sheweth the ungodly world a true picture of Christ's church in all purity."

Rebecca had thought on that, and she had read and reread Ephesians 5:21–33 and 1 Peter 3:1–9.

Alone in her room that evening she had written:

Dear Adam,

My letter to you on Friday was, I fear, written in haste and perhaps motivated by pride in desiring to show you that I am wholly committed to the Lord. Since writing that letter, I have been in much distress of soul and trouble of mind.

How could Christian women, such as our minister's wife, Mrs. Baxter, or the godly wives of the Bible, be fully committed to the Lord and yet at the same time be totally committed to their husbands (as I wish to be, if the Lord ever permits me to marry), I asked myself.

Then I heard Pastor Baxter preach on how Christian husband-wife relationships show Christ's love and compassion for His church to our neighbors. This caused me to think that perhaps Paul in First Corinthians was talking about a special class of women (or men!) who may not need to marry, but that most women (and men!) do bring glory to God by marrying and living together in holiness and godliness. So, if God wants me to marry, I shall marry, but only if He shows me clearly to do so.

Adam, I hope this letter isn't confusing or presumptuous, since my intention is merely to clear up any misunderstandings in the last one.

Yours affectionately,
Rebecca

Rebecca didn't know if she was the more troubled with having written Adam twice before he wrote her again. "You'll think I am forward for writing you so often," she had written, but she had torn this up and rewritten the letter, since he *might* think she was forward from the mere power of suggestion. Or was she writing too much about marriage—two letters in a row! Or he might be offended simply by the large number of letters she was writing!

The next letter that troubled Rebecca was her note to him which contained an announcement that the Young People's Fellowship of Tory Hill Church planned a St. Valentine's Day party for the second Friday night in February. The members of the Fellowship would meet at eight o'clock at the brick house, and "weather permitting," all would go to the millpond to skate and enjoy Christian fellowship around a bonfire. As things turned out, this announcement and its accompanying letter were to be overshadowed by an event so shocking that Rebecca could not long worry about offending Adam.

Two dozen invitations had been carefully inked by Mrs. Baxter on card stock, and these were handed out to any members of the group who might wish to invite a guest. Rebecca did not desire to be brash about inviting Adam to a young people's skating party, even though Mrs. Baxter had stressed that the party was for "anyone under thirty and unmarried." Should a woman ask a man to a party, she pondered. Still, how *would* Adam know about the party if she did not send the invitation? Furthermore, she knew by his last letter that he planned to take an early afternoon train from Boston to Maine some Friday soon.

So the Tuesday before the party Rebecca mailed off the invitation with a brief note of her own.

On Friday afternoon the phone rang; it was Adam. "May I have the honor of the company of Miss Rebecca Randall at the skating party planned by the Young People's Church Fellowship tonight at eight?" his deep voice rumbled teasingly, so strong that even the telephone's flat modulation could not hide either his masculinity or his pleasure at being invited.

"I'll be ready—delighted!" Rebecca was taken by surprise to hear his voice phoning from Aunt Mary Ladd's in North Riverboro. There was much she wished to say to Adam, but this was all she could utter, except to inform him that John and Mark were even now shoveling the ice and hauling logs for a bonfire.

The party was a success—to a point. Several teens had griped that they were being prevented from skating on the best ice. John and Mark had cleared the snow from much of the small, upper pond with their shovels, and it was on this pond, used in dry fall weather as a reservoir for backup water power to keep the sawmill running all year, that they would skate.

The large, lower pond, held back by the main dam beside the mill, had been used for skating until the snow covered it in January. The ground was now frozen, and the flowage of the Saco was reduced to a trickle. Since the mill operator had drained the lower pond to turn his wheel and power his saw and planer, the ice on the lower pond had caved in like a rotted barn roof, and great cakes had until recently lain like beached whales on the frozen mud.

Nearly a week earlier, however, the mill operator had shut the spillway and sent his crew to work cutting logs in the woods. Gradually a trickle of water from beneath the snow filled the pond, slowly, surely backing up as new ice formed among the floating cakes. A slick, snowless expanse of black ice now spread across the lower pond, making a broader and far more appealing surface to skate upon than the rough spot on the upper pond that Mark and John had been able to clear. Pastor Baxter had strictly admonished all the young people to stay off this new ice. "It won't be safe for at least a week, maybe two," he had said.

❧ ❧ ❧

"Mr. Baxter, Seth Strout has had a stroke. The doctor's there right now, an' they need you soon's you can get there." It was Aunt Jane, who had trudged through the snow to the millpond after taking the urgent phone call.

"Mr. Ladd," said Parson Baxter, turning to Adam before he and Mrs. Baxter hurried off to their horse and cutter for the drive to Strouts, "Will you and Rebecca take charge, please? I see that you have brought your guitar, and so these kids can sing for a while before you dismiss them with a prayer. We'll not have the Bible lesson, but the Lord knows about that."

Later, Adam pushed the half-burned logs onto the coals, then he arranged several large rocks around the flames while Rebecca set to work mixing the chocolate syrup she had prepared beforehand into the milk in a copper kettle. "Give me a hand, here, please, Adam," she called. Together they positioned the kettle over the flames, and with a wooden spoon Rebecca stirred the mixture to keep it from scorching.

During a moment's rest from working over the smoky fire, she took stock of the figures gliding in the shadows over the moonlit pond. The milk she had brought would scarcely supply enough hot chocolate to go round once, she realized. She couldn't send Adam for more—he was needed to chaperone, Rebecca's common sense told her. And John was obviously the protector and sustainer of Persis Watson at the moment.

Then, with a shower of ice, Mark braked to a stop beside her. "We need another gallon of milk as soon as you can get it, Mark," Rebecca said, holding up the empty pail and its snap lid.

"Sure thing." He grabbed the pail and was off.

"Where's Mark?" It was Thirza Meserve. She had been more or less flitting about all evening, doing figure eights and whatever else would impress the crowd since she had attained no small ability on figure skates.

"Gone to the house for more milk," replied Rebecca without looking up from her stirring.

"The dear boy promised to skate with little ol' me soon's he finished racing with the fellows."

Rebecca ignored her.

"Well, if that's the Randall way of treating friends, I'll find my friends elsewhere!"

"Don't take it so hard," said Rebecca merrily but evenly. "You're young yet!"

Without another word Thirza disappeared into the darkness in the direction of the other skaters.

Presently Mark appeared with the milk. "Someone's skating on the lower pond, and I think it's probably Thirza," he said with agitation as he set the bucket down.

"Pastor Baxter made a point of saying no one is to go on the lower pond." Rebecca was apprehensive and angry.

"Thirza said she was goin' home if I didn't hurry up an' skate with her. I guess she's kept her threat," Mark answered flippantly.

"Thirza lives just beyond the sawmill, directly across the pond," Rebecca remembered aloud. Then, "Oh, no!" she shrieked, "if she's heading for the dam, she'll go through—the ice is barely frozen next to the spillway. Mark, we've got to stop her!" Shouting to Adam to follow, Rebecca ducked into the thicket separating the upper and lower ponds. She soon popped out on the other side, but Thirza was not to be seen. The three circled the ice, following the shore. Mark raced ahead, leaving Adam to aid Rebecca, who had twice stumbled through the thin ice into knee-deep water as she tried to avoid the stumps and large rocks along the shoreline. In the moonlight, shadows became obstacles and real obstacles were invisible until it was too late to avoid them.

"There she is! Thirza's gone through, but she's hanging on." Mark, realizing that he could not immediately reach her, paused, waiting for Rebecca and Adam to catch up with him. Then gathering his wits, he dove for a pile of boards, and in seconds he returned with the widest one he could lay his hands on. He skated several yards toward Thirza, who was keeping her head up by clutching the edge of the ice near the dam where she had broken through.

Mark then lay on his stomach and began to scramble along the ice, pushing the board ahead of him. "*Don't* let go of the board, Mark," Adam cautioned.

John and the others had by now gathered around Rebecca and Adam, and John was carrying one of the kerosene lanterns which had been used to mark off the ice for the skaters. "Adam, there's a rope hanging just inside the mill," cried John, who had had business there on a trip for Squire Bean.

"For heaven's sake, go get it, man!"

John was off at a run.

"Rebecca, I'm going out on the dam! Have John toss me that rope through the window in the mill when he finds it." Turning to the group of young people behind him, he commanded, "Nobody goes on this ice. And do what Rebecca says without arguing." Adam ran to the dam, and climbing the rock-filled log wall next to it, he sat on the concrete and hacked through the frozen laces of his skates with his pocketknife, hurling them up on shore and throwing his coat after them. He dropped his gloves while taking off his coat, but he made no attempt to find them.

Mark had nearly reached Thirza by now. Then, "Thirz," he cried, "I can't get any closer because the ice is cracking under me. Here! hang onto this." With that, he gave the board a shove, and Thirza let go of the ice and wrapped both arms around the board as it shot by her, leaving her bobbing in the icy water with the board as a tenacious buoy. Fortunately, she was drifting toward Adam.

Whether it was Thirza's sudden shift of weight, Mark's thrust in pushing the board to her, or a combination, no one could say. But the thin sheet of ice under Mark suddenly tilted, and Mark slipped head first under the ice which Thirza had been clutching.

"O-o-o-o-o-o-o-o-h-h!" from the crowd of young people.

"Mark!" screamed Rebecca.

Jenny and Fanny, who had been hugging each other, began to sob in unison.

Adam, on the dam, carefully moved to a point above Thirza, then he grabbed the rope which John had tied to a beam inside and lowered from the mill window above the dam. Adam wrapped the rope under his arms and knotted it carefully. Ted Perkins, who had followed Adam's example in cutting himself out of his skates' frozen laces, was crawling along the ice-coated dam toward Adam.

Adam slid into the pond amid the floating ice and swam to Thirza, who, no sooner than he grabbed her hair, fainted from the cold and lost her grip on the board. "Haul away, John," he shouted. John and Ted pulled the shadowy figures to the dam, as Adam kicked and struggled to keep Thirza's head up. "John, you keep that rope taut while Ted gets a firm grip—Ted, don't try to pull either of us out until John is down here to help you." Adam spoke in the calm, even voice he was used to using in dealing with Boston businessmen. The younger men, catching courage from his self-control, obeyed him at once. For the moment, Adam could not allow himself to think of Mark.

"All right, pull Thirza out and carry her to high ground," Adam commanded. Ted dragged Thirza to shore, and John, after hauling Adam out, tied the rope around himself and dived in after his brother. Adam, shivering and shaking, tried to help John by playing the rope out as John swam.

By now Ted was back on the dam with Adam's coat. Adam struggled into his overcoat, and he and Ted helplessly watched as John exhausted himself, diving and plunging beneath the ice for Mark. When at last John was unable to continue and it looked as though he might drown also, Adam and Ted hauled him back onto the dam.

"Let go of me! Let me go!" John rasped, struggling to free himself from Adam and Ted as they dragged him onto the snow-covered shore. "I'm going back for Mark!"

Adam, himself near collapse, released his grip, and he and John fell together in the snow. Gathering his strength, Adam then embraced John, pinning his arms to his sides. "Mark is gone," he cried. "You've done your best. I've got to see to it that we don't have another drowning here tonight—-do you understand me, man?"

John crumpled in a heap, sobbing, "I couldn't reach you, Mark; I couldn't reach you, Mark, oh, Mark!"

"Have we lost Mark?" Rebecca now clutched Adam, fighting to keep from becoming hysterical.

"Yes, Mark is gone," Adam replied. "Thirza, at least, has a chance."

"But . . . but can't *somebody* try again . . . once more, at least?" Rebecca cried.

"I'm sorry," Adam answered firmly. "Mark is drowned; he's been under far too long to be found alive. My responsibility right now is to prevent any more drownings. We'll search for his body again by daylight."

Adam gathered the unconscious Thirza into his arms, and with a firm "Let's go, folks," he strode toward the brick house. Rebecca and John, hugging their younger sisters close, came along behind, as Ted herded the younger members of the group toward the road with strict instructions to go straight home.

"Gracious," cried Aunt Jane, meeting the young folks at the door, "did she hurt herself—why, she's all wet, and so's John!"

"Here, lay her on my bed," cried Aurelia, swinging open the door to the downstairs bedroom which had become hers upon moving into the brick house. Aunt Jane and Aurelia went to work at once, undressing Thirza, wrapping her in hot towels, rubbing her until she regained consciousness.

Rebecca phoned Thirza's parents and Mrs. Meserve soon arrived. She then called Aurelia aside and told her that Mark had not been saved. Though she still walked with a cane, Aurelia was determined to run at once to the pond where Mark had last been seen alive sliding under the ice. Rebecca was able to restrain her mother only long enough for Adam, who was now wearing John's extra union suit and overalls, to pull his boots on. Slipping back into his overcoat, he and John helped Aurelia pick her way over the frozen, rutted path to the sawmill.

Ted Perkins and his father, blacksmith Bill Perkins, were at the mill when Adam and John returned with Aurelia. Mr. Perkins assured Aurelia that he would find the mill operator and have the pond drained at once, though "It'll be morning, at least, before we can see the bottom," he said. Not surprisingly, Adam and John were obliged to take turns carrying the distraught, fainting Aurelia much of the way home in their arms.

Rebecca, for her part, spent the evening consoling her younger sisters. "Mark is with Jesus," she told them simply. Big sister and younger girls all forgot that they were "big girls now," as they had so often been reminded by Aurelia. Adam spent much of the night stoking the stoves with coal and oak, quietly caring for tasks which the Randalls had neglected during the long, cold evening of weeping. None undressed for bed that night; the girls and women merely collapsed fully clothed on their beds when finally they were exhausted.

When Rebecca tiptoed into the sitting room just before daybreak, she found Adam, still in John's overalls, slouched in the Morris chair, where he had managed to sleep for a couple of hours. He struggled to his feet as she approached. "What will we do if we can't find Mark?" she wept, collapsing sobbing into his arms. "And what will Mother do?" Adam held her close, and the heaving of his chest told Rebecca that he was sobbing also.

"Mark . . . Mark is with the Lord," said Adam. Though she herself had told her younger sisters that the evening before, Rebecca had not been ready to really accept it. "We can only give his body a decent burial, now," Adam went on gently, but refusing to mince his words.

"But . . . but how will you find it?" Rebecca was conscious of making herself refer to her brother's body as "it," rather than "him."

"That shouldn't be a problem. The millpond is being drained, and as soon as it's fully light, I'm sure we can find the body." Adam and John dressed and went off to find the mill owner, who had promised to meet them at the dam at daybreak.

❧ ❧ ❧

"Why, Mother, *why* did Mark have to die? With John going to college this fall, you need him *so!*" Rebecca's voice contained no trace of bitterness as she queried her mother on Monday afternoon after the funeral. Rather, the anguish of having a beloved brother snatched so suddenly and apparently so senselessly came through in her plaint. Mark's funeral had been the most solemn, sobering experience Riverboro had experienced in many a year. Mark's body had been temporarily laid in the crypt beneath Tory Hill to await spring at Sunnybrook, come April, and the villagers had wended their way home to return to their rounds of duties. Though the St. Valentine's Day drowning had been shocking, most dwellers in this tiny hamlet would return to their lives on the morrow little touched beyond the shock of the moment.

But things would never be the same at the brick house, Rebecca knew. "God's purposes are past finding out until He is ready to reveal them, my dear," Aurelia, now the comforter, said quietly. "Don't blame Thirza; headstrong child that she is, the Lord will deal with her in His time. It may be that the life that has been so suddenly snatched from our home will arise in her to the glory of the Lord.

She has the beginnings of a woman whom God can use, if only her determination is given some direction."

"We can only forgive Thirza," interrupted Adam, who had walked into the sitting room at the moment Aurelia and Rebecca were discussing the accidental drowning. "She acted foolishly and against Mr. Baxter's instructions to stay off the ice of the lower pond, to be sure. But she did not cause Mark's death, though he died trying to save her. Mark's death was an act of Him who is the giver and taker of life, I'm afraid."

"But when will it end?" cried Rebecca, still unconsoled. "We lost Father, then Mira. Aunt Miranda died before her time."

"Our times are in God's hands," said Adam. "For some He gives but a moment; others a day, or a year; some live out their three score and ten years, and others may live that and half again."

"That's the lesson of Job, isn't it," said Rebecca.

"It is indeed. Meanwhile, we who remain must go on living," concluded Adam.

"You're right, of course," Rebecca responded, drying her eyes. "I know that already I have been made the stronger through the loss of several of my family. I guess God isn't through with me yet," she said, smiling.

Rebecca buried her face in Adam's chest as he patted her head. "I remember the afternoon at Emily Maxwell's apartment when you showed me that cameo portrait of your mother, how my heart went out to your sorrow then. Now you have wept in mine. I have lost a brother; Mother has lost a son—can I gain in you a friend?"

Aurelia limped into the kitchen, leaving Adam to answer Rebecca without eavesdroppers. Though Adam left that evening for North Riverboro, where he would journey back to Boston and his business on the morrow, Rebecca slept soundly that night, more soundly than she had slept in weeks. She dreamed not of Mark, though she had dreamed of him for the three nights previous; she dreamed of children who crowded around her, of children who needed to be loved, of children who needed her. And she dreamed of Adam, strong, ready, leading her in time of deepest need.

That night Adam wrote from his room at Aunt Mary's:

> Dear Rebecca,
>
> It suddenly occurs to me that I have not answered your last letter. May I say that I enjoyed the skating party very much, though of course none of us were happy with the ending. I felt more wanted and needed as a guest in the brick house than I have for as long as I can remember. I hope that once you have sorted out your sorrows and your joys, you'll want to see more of me, who am but sorry company, I'm afraid.
>
> With Fondest Regards,
> Adam

14

A BARN WEDDING

"Doctor Adams's commencement address was the most cynical speech I have ever heard!" Rebecca, seated in the platform rocker in the sitting room, waited for Abijah Flagg's answer.

"Henry Adams was a guest lecturer at Bowdoin College last semester, and I was not happy to have him bring the address at my graduation," Abijah confessed, agreeing with Rebecca's outspoken opinion. "He certainly lacks the patriotism of his ancestors."

"Our little Decoration Day parade this morning surely shows that patriotism is alive and well in our corner of America," Emma Jane interrupted.

"I'm afraid Doctor Adams wouldn't appreciate our brand of patriotic activity," said Abijah, whose education had left him wiser about the world than Emma's limited high school training. "Though Adams's ancestors are counted among the founders of American freedom, he apparently believes, that like Holmes's *Chambered Nautilus,* he's outgrown such simple concepts as love of one's country."

"How about love of one's man?" giggled Emma, clutching Abijah's arm. "We've got a wedding coming up!"

"Wedding? Whose? When?" Abijah spoke in mock ignorance, then he stifled a very real yawn. "To tell you ladies the truth, I haven't had time to think about weddings. With final exams, two term papers to finish, and graduation last Saturday, and with job interviews in between, I've been surviving on three hours' sleep a night."

"Well, you just stretch out on the davenport and sleep, dear, 'cause Becky an' I have an appointment upstairs with Aunt Jane to pin my weddin' dress up so's she can finish sewin' it."

"Sure you don't mind? I could use a nap," he said to Rebecca, almost pleading.

"Not at all. We won't disturb you."

"Have you got a bootjack by the back door?" Abijah inquired. "I don't think you want me to nap on your couch with my boots on."

"I'll pull 'em off for you." Emma Jane jumped to her feet and grasped one of Abijah's well-blacked walking boots in both her hands.

"You'll be sorry you tried. They're on pretty tight."

"Don't be silly!"

"Okay. Heave ho!" Abijah grabbed onto the arm of the davenport and braced himself with his other foot. The boot came off, all right, and Emma Jane went sprawling on her back on the braided rug.

"Just what we needed—a little drama to liven up our day," Rebecca chuckled, as Abijah, who only laughed at Emma's folly, tackled his other boot with both hands.

"Do you *always* wear such tight boots?" inquired Emma in disgust. "You can't use the excuse that you're a growing boy any longer!"

Abijah turned one of them over. "New soles for graduation—and for the wedding; see, I haven't forgotten. The cobbler pinched the sides in too much when he stitched the soles on. If they don't stretch out in a week or so, I'm going to have to buy a new pair from my first pay at Cooper, Drake, & Parmenter's law office in Maplewood."

"Em said you were looking into a job as a law clerk," said Rebecca. "Then it's certain?"

"It sure is—I've got my contract already!"

An hour and a half later, when Rebecca and Emma Jane returned to the sitting room—after much pinning and tucking seams and hems and adjusting whalebone hoops, with cries of, "You'll have to lose more weight," and squeals of, "Oh, it'll never be done in time for the wedding"—they found Abijah stretched totally limp on the couch snoring loudly. "Wedding music," chuckled Rebecca. "A week of that and you'll want to trade him off for a noiseless number."

"I'm sure I won't," said Emma, who seldom saw humor in Rebecca's continual wisecracking. "But what's this?" Emma picked up an open photo album which Abijah had laid on the floor as he dozed off. "Hey, here's an *outdoor* photo in this old album," said Emma, who was accustomed to only stiff, formal portraits in photo albums. "It looks like—it is!—the front of your barn, Becky, and the doors are open. I'd never seen your barn doors open until your brothers put Dick-Boy and Molly in there. But say, there's a picnic going on! Who are all those people?" She passed the album to Rebecca. Half a dozen young women and four of middle age stood stiffly behind long plank tables built on sawhorses and loaded with food in the open barn doors. Two men, one elderly and one past middle age, were seated on ladder-back chairs in the foreground, and two younger men stood beside them. With the men was a withered-up, toothless, ancient woman leaning on a hand-carved cane. Perhaps a dozen children, most of them barefoot urchins, were seated cross-legged on the grass in front of their elders. A lace-bordered blur appeared in the photo where an infant, unable to sit still for the time-exposure photo, had tumbled over; a second blur, this one furry, was evidently a cat or a small dog. In the background, next to one open barn door, was a peddler's wagon with "W. F. Fuller, Photographer" neatly lettered on the side.

"Certainly you recognize several of the younger women – three of them, for sure," Rebecca said pleasantly as she passed the album back to Emma Jane.

"That's . . . why, that's your Aunt Miranda." Emma Jane pointed at a woman whose face had a take-charge demeanor. Her arms were folded, and she stood with a carving knife behind a roast on the table.

"Good! Keep looking."

"Well, I see your mother and Aunt Jane."

"That was a Sawyer family reunion on the Fourth of July. They had them every year until Grandfather Sawyer died. The other women are my mother's cousins," explained Rebecca. "The dignified looking gentleman is my grandfather, who died shortly before I was born, and the old man is his father, my great-grandpa. The old, old lady with the cane is Grandfather Sawyer's grandmother, Albanah Sawyer – she was born in 1763, just at the close of the French and Indian War right after her mother learned that Albanah's father had fallen in battle. She lived to be past a hundred. Great-grandmother Albanah and her husband were the first settlers in this part of the valley. He was in the Continental Army during the Revolution, and he took his mustering-out pay in Maine forest land which he cleared by himself, so Aunt Miranda always said."

By this time Abijah was awake and sitting up. "You girls have been looking at the *people* in that picture. I've been looking at the *barn*."

"What do you mean?" Emma Jane was puzzled.

"Well, we're planning a noon wedding at the meeting-house, then planning to drive the whole hungry crowd down here for the reception in the brick house's parlor, since yours is too small, Emma. That's two miles to traipse with a crowd—it'll look like a circus parade. So why don't we have a barn wedding right here—the barn was good enough for the Sawyers' reunion. Since you live just across the bridge, it'd be a lot more convenient, all around."

"We—ell," Emma hesitated, "it makes no difference to me, just so's we get married properly. But how will we ever get it cleaned up and decorated?"

"I don't see any problem with that," enthused Rebecca. "We've already put Molly out to pasture for the summer—she's dry, anyway, until she has her calf this fall. I'm sure we can borrow a stall for Dick-Boy at Cobbs for a few days while we air out his stall. John plans to sweep all the old chaff and hay out to get the barn clean as a whistle before we put in a few bales for the cow and horse for the winter, anyway."

"Say," said Emma, "I remember how hard we worked getting ready for graduation at Wareham Academy—only I didn't get to graduate," she added in a quiet, little voice. "I guess I could've passed Latin if 'Bijah, here, had been around to help me translate, 'stead 'o just writing me Latin letters." She patted his arm and giggled.

"We went through bushels and bushels of balsam fir cuttings, just to decorate the hall for the party after graduation," Rebecca remembered, wistfully recalling that she had missed the party when she learned that Aunt Miranda had had a stroke.

"Well, *I* want balsam fir this time," said Emma boldly. "It's *my* wedding, and I'm sure not going to flunk out this time. But I'll need help. I'm sure I can get my brother, Ted, to cut fir branches in the woods."

"I can borrow Squire Bean's team of horses to help Ted—can we use your grandfather's old hayrack to haul the boughs from the woods, Rebecca?" asked Abijah.

"Sure you can. But the hardest job will be making those fir-tip walls. There are literally millions of tips to snip off with shears and poke in a chicken-wire frame. We don't have a senior class to do the work this time, but I think I can enlist Jenny and Fanny if I bribe 'em with a plate of cookies now and then," Rebecca responded. "But where are we ever going to get enough chicken wire?"

"That's easy," squealed Emma, now thoroughly enthusiastic about a barn wedding—for with Rebecca involved, what could go wrong?—"We have rolls and rolls of it in the shed behind Father's blacksmith shop. We bought our place ten years ago from a man who used to raise chickens. Father and Ted tore the fences down, and the wire has been stored ever since."

❧ ❧ ❧

Saturday, June 15 came, and no brighter day could there have been for a Riverboro wedding. Under Rebecca's direction preparations had gone well, but not without a few setbacks. Rebecca had herself hung chicken wire on small nails from a hay scaffold directly behind the platform John Randall and Ted Perkins had built for a stage. Fanny and Jenny had spent two days poking balsam tips into a huge wire drape, and Rebecca and Emma Jane had helped with the tedious process for several hours each. Even Aurelia and Mrs. Perkins had poked tips into the numberless holes in the wire netting.

The great, green drape was three quarters completed, and small Fanny was sitting atop an eight-foot stepladder poking tips into wire loops, when without warning, the entire backdrop curtain let go, and Fanny was pinned underneath. It required Rebecca, Jenny, Aunt Jane, and Aurelia to pull the heavy drape of wire and fir off Fanny, who, except for bruised elbows, fortunately was unhurt, since she had landed in a pile of fir tips on the floor. The mess was left until John and Abijah could assess the damage, and it soon appeared that most of the fallen section would have to be done over—this time nailed securely onto extra slats at John's direction.

"What could you expect," John said indignantly, when he saw the few small nails his older sister had hung the wire on. "That thing must weigh half a ton. It was a disaster waiting to happen!"

"Let's be glad it didn't come down durin' the weddin'," Aunt Jane remarked, playing the peacemaker.

Emma's father, Bill Perkins, her brother, Ted, and Abijah Flagg helped John Randall trundle the old Steinway piano from the brick house's sitting room, through the long ell, and into the barn. Though Rebecca was the maid of honor, she had been designated pianist for the solo numbers preceding the ceremony; Mrs. Baxter would then render Wagner's "Lohengrin" for the wedding march. The day before the wedding Rebecca had been practicing with Huldah Meserve, who, home from Lewiston where she worked as an office secretary, was designated soloist.

"This piano's dreadfully out of tune, Rebecca. We simply *must* get another one."

"It is, for sure," agreed Rebecca helplessly. "But it was okay yesterday when Mr. Perkins and the fellows moved it out here."

"You should know well enough that when you move a piano, you may have to retune it," Huldah haughtily countered. Rebecca had known, of course, that such problems could occur; but the likelihood of it actually happening had not entered her optimistic mind.

"What'll we do?" wailed Emma Jane, who had come to the barn from a last-minute dress-fitting session in the house with Aunt Jane.

"Don't fret your silly head about it. That's *our* responsibility," said Rebecca firmly, taking Emma's arm and marching her back through the ell toward the house, as Huldah trailed along behind, fussing and complaining. "I've got an idea," Rebecca confided, though she had no idea what that idea was until the three of them reached the kitchen and she spied the telephone on the wall.

"It'd better be a good idea," put in Huldah, never the one to try to smooth things over when the pot could more easily be kept boiling.

"Wait for me in the sitting room," said Rebecca firmly, motioning toward the hall door as they entered the kitchen from the ell. Huldah quickly disappeared into the hall, but Emma Jane lingered by the door as Rebecca raised the receiver from the wall telephone's cradle. There was no one on their party line, so holding the cradle down with a finger, she gave the crank on the oak box several vigorous turns.

"Central," answered the operator. It was Aunt Sarah Cobb.

"Aunt Sarah, can you get me Wareham Academy? It's more or less an emergency."

"That's long distance, you know, Becky—more'n ten miles and out of our district."

"I know it's long distance. Please put me through."

"Father will pay for the phone call, if it will get our piano tuned," Emma Jane whispered across the kitchen. "He'll pay whatever it costs to get a piano tuner over here," she added, having by now guessed Rebecca's intent.

As things turned out, the phone call to Wareham's music department elicited the information that an excellent piano tuner, an elderly blind man, lived on the road between Riverboro and Wareham, only seven or eight miles distant. Two hours later, after Abijah had made a buggy trip to the old gentleman's house, the piano was being tuned, and the work was done in time for Rebecca and Huldah to practice after the rehearsal that evening.

Emma Jane Perkins made a beautiful bride, despite her protestations about her "impossible" strawberry blonde hair. She even managed to disguise her few freckles with strategically placed rouge and powder. And Aunt Jane, whose abilities as a seamstress—though she lacked imagination as to style—had helped many a Riverboro maiden as a bride or bridesmaid, prevented Emma from trying to stuff her well-proportioned size ten figure into a size eight wedding dress. "Iffen I was to stitch the seams where you want 'em, Emma Jane," Aunt Jane had said one day as she was tucking and fitting, letting out and taking in, "you'd need a team o' workhosses to pull your corset strings tight enough t' git ye into the dress. More brides faint durin' the weddin' ceremony from vanity than from fear o' marryin'," she warned.

The songs were sung, the vows exchanged, the prayers offered; Parson Baxter pronounced the happy couple man and wife, the blushing bride was kissed; the rice was thrown, the bouquet tossed. Like a million brides before and a million more since, Emma Jane could not resist plastering her groom's face with wedding cake and frosting in front of a hundred appreciative guests. Thirza Meserve and

Fanny Randall, given the responsibility of unwrapping the gifts, neatly packed all the tags into an envelope without writing the contents of each package on the tags' backs—creating a mystery which took Mrs. Perkins two days on the phone to unravel.

One gift, however, needed no explanation. A pair of new cordovan leather boots for the groom was left unwrapped, but a note in verse was tucked deep inside, which fortunately the girls did not remove:

These boots are yours
and yours alone
To walk the roads
of sand or stone;

So walk a mile
and think of me,
And weary feet
will comfort see.

R. R. R.

When Rebecca was at last assured that her mother and aunt had the distribution of berry pies, coffee, and hand-cranked ice cream well under way, and that she was no longer needed to direct Ted Perkins, John, and Jenny in their interminable errands—"John, we need another block of ice from the icehouse"; "Ted, *please* keep turning that freezer crank, or the dasher'll stick to the side and the ice cream will be lumpy"; "Jenny, two more pies from the cellar, please"—she signaled Uncle Jerry to bring his team around.

And such a team it was! Uncle Jerry's coach horses, still in regular use with a younger driver, made their weekly runs to Maplewood depot and post office, since no through trains ran through Riverboro. These stalwart steeds were now hitched to Deacon Israel Sawyer's old two-seater surrey, gussied up with a new top of leather dyed red—Rebecca's inspiration of course—new paint, and freshly varnished spokes. John had begun the restoration of the vehicle a week earlier, planning to hitch it single-harness to Dick-Boy. But when it became evident that he had not enough time to re-rig the old conveyance by the wedding day, he asked, and was gladly given, permission to use the coach horses.

Adam Ladd, at his Aunt Mary's for a week, had put in an appearance at the brick house the day before the wedding, just in time to varnish the surrey's spokes. It was not by coincidence, he later admitted to Rebecca, that he chose to take a vacation the week of Emma's wedding.

But the wagon need not have been painted, Emma realized, as Uncle Jerry drew up to the barn door. The spokes of its wheels were interwoven with strips of red bunting, and the surrey's box was completely hung with chicken wire netting and balsam, like the barn's interior. The young people, led by Ted, wasted no time in tying tin cans to the rear of the wagon as Adam handed Rebecca, clutching purse and sweater, up into the front passenger seat. He then took the reins from Uncle Jerry and held the horses while the guests of honor clambered aboard—Emma Jane, still in her silk wedding dress, and Abijah, looking awkward in a swallow-tailed coat and top hat.

A cheer went up from the guests as Adam paraded the horses in front of the barn and out the circle drive. A slap of the reins and a "Hup!" and the team broke into a trot as it hit the bridge under the hill, cans bouncing merrily along the planks. Bowser, the Perkins's English foxhound, hearing the racket and seeing his mistress leaving in such a noisy manner, barked and nipped at the horses' heels until Adam drew the rig up and Emma Jane comforted him and sent him home—a circumstance which drew shouts of "You've sent the wrong one home!" from guests still watching on the brick house's lawn.

Abijah instructed Adam to turn in to the squire's yard near the top of the hill on the road to Maplewood. Disentangling himself from Emma Jane's possessive grip, the embarrassed groom disappeared, his tails bounding like a squirrel's as he hurried through the woodshed door. Presently his head appeared from an upstairs window. "I've got to change my c-c-clothes," he stammered. "Squire's gotta mail this borrowed monkey suit back to Bowdoin College on M-M-Monday."

Abijah soon reappeared at the shed door, this time dressed in a business suit. Halfway to the surrey he stopped, smacked his hands together, and raced back inside. When he came out the second time he was carrying a large leather valise. "'All my worldly possessions I thee endow,' and they're all in here," he mumbled, cramming the satchel under the seat with Emma's suitcase, which had been stored there since early that morning. Hopping aboard he cried, "Let's go!"

The shadows were long in the late spring afternoon when Adam drew the surrey and horses up at the door of a neat, Dutch bungalow which Abijah and Emma Jane had rented on a side street in Maplewood. "When will we see you again?" Rebecca inquired of Emma, as Adam helped Abijah pry the suitcases and a couple of boxes loose from under the seats.

"Week after next, by Sunday for sure," Emma said. "We're taking the afternoon train to Old Orchard Beach tomorrow, where 'Bijah's got us a cottage for a week. Then after we come back here and unpack, we'll take the coach over to Riverboro and move the rest of our things here with Father's team. Abijah's got to start his new job the first of July." Emma hugged Rebecca and kissed her cheek fervently. "Have fun on the way back to Riverboro."

"Certainly," was all the ordinarily loquacious Rebecca could murmur, as Abijah swept Emma up and strode toward the open door of their home.

"There, we won't have to listen to those anymore," Adam said with an air of finality, as with his pocketknife he snipped the last of the cans from the wagon just outside the village of Maplewood. Rebecca, who had been tearing the last of the tattered bunting off the surrey's wheels, hopped into her seat without waiting for Adam to boost her. He jumped in, and with a cluck to the horses and a slap of the reins, they were off for Riverboro.

Rebecca shut herself up to her thoughts for a long, long time. She had traveled this very road once as a child, behind these same horses, now grown old. It was a new life she had been facing that long-ago May day, when in Uncle Jeremiah's stagecoach she had bounced along in silence, until with a poke of her parasol she had insisted he let her ride in the driver's seat with him.

Little had changed along this old road. New dogs were in the yards; a farmer had replaced his hand pump with a windmill; a sturdy old maple had been felled to let the telephone lines through—that was all.

Nor was there now mystery in where she was going. At the end of her journey, she knew, was the brick house, faithful Aunt Jane, Mother, brother John, and her sisters. Rebecca was now the mistress of the brick house, and she was troubled as she contemplated again the responsibility that this entailed. Her trouble turned to agitation as she thought on the long task of cleaning up after Emma's wedding, a task which must begin early Monday morning after a brief Sabbath rest on the morrow. Impatient, impetuous Rebecca! Had not Aunt Miranda taught her the virtue of sticking to a task to its conclusion, she might have remained "all Randall" to her regret.

At the end of this road, also, was a career, which would begin in just two months. True, she would go on her way to Portland before the job actually began. Where this career would lead, Rebecca had not a clue. Close-folded in the mind of God, she knew her future rested.

Within, however, Rebecca was a much different person from the little girl who had traveled that road with Uncle Jerry years earlier. The twig had been bent; the sapling had been pruned; the roots of the growing plant had been watered and fed; the branches had spread forth their leaves to the Son above all suns, until like "a tree planted by the rivers of water," Rebecca's season was ready to "bring forth its fruit."

The rattle of the surrey wheels on the gravel highway and the clip-clop of the heavy hooves on the grassy strip in the middle came through to Rebecca's consciousness just as they crested a grade. A hundred miles to the west the White Mountains ranged in their glory along the horizon, as the purple, pink, and lavender rays of the setting sun spread along the streamers of clouds now stretching into the evening sky.

She clutched Adam's elbow. "Oh, Mr. Aladdin, dear Adam, it's so beautiful," Rebecca murmured at last.

"It is indeed," he agreed. "Some folks, unfortunately, seldom look high enough to enjoy the sunset."

"I heard a speech last month by Doctor Adams, an intellectual whom I think must never have seen a sunset," responded Rebecca.

"At Abijah's graduation—Bowdoin College?"

"Yes. And what a disappointment!"

"And what an agreeable circumstance to find in you a young lady, though with only an academy education, who can understand enough of Henry Brooks Adams to disagree with him. A lot of college graduates can't do as much!"

The miles rolled by, and it was quite dark by the time Rebecca and Adam approached Riverboro. As they began the descent of the long grade ending at the bridge into the village, the moon appeared over the western horizon, orange and huge above the mountains. Adam turned the horses off the highway into a pair of wagon ruts which led to the sawmill at the head of the lower millpond, just upstream from Bill Perkins's smithy. Presently they arrived at a point where the road followed the shoreline. Adam tied the horses to an elm, then he helped Rebecca from the carriage.

Hand clasped in hand, the couple walked, picking their way down a steep path to the edge of the small lake, where Adam directed Rebecca to a lichen-covered granite boulder. Rebecca curled up on the gray stone in the moonlight, drawing her slippered feet under the pink silk skirt of the bridesmaid's dress she still wore, hugging her sweater tight about her shoulders against the evening chill. She rested her chin on Adam's shoulder as he leaned on the rock beside her.

"Perhaps I shouldn't have brought you here again," Adam proposed after a long silence.

"I wanted to come back."

"I only mean to say that if you find it painful, we can go somewhere else. The last time I was out on that dam was a night I don't like to think about." Adam turned briefly toward the sawmill casting its shadow over the lake's head. "I'm truly sorry—it just never occurred to me that it *is* the same place until I saw the mill in the moonlight—I mean, it doesn't seem like the same place in the spring."

"You don't need to apologize," Rebecca murmured softly. "Mark is gone, and I accept that. Oh, the pain comes back once in a while when I think of his pranks, and how he was growing to be such a man. But this old mill holds no regrets for me. I used to come here often to watch the men haul the logs inside with horses, and more than once I've been scolded by Aunt Miranda for sitting too long on a log pile watching the sawyer cut pine trees into boards, making me late for supper. How angry she'd get," Rebecca laughed, "when after scolding me I'd say, 'Auntie, you're a Sawyer an' I'm half Sawyer; Sawyers should be interested in watchin' sawyers work, shouldn't they?'"

Long the couple watched the moon rise over the lake and listened to the trill of the peepers along the shore and the distant rush of the waterfall below. Adam slapped a mosquito. "Pesky critters. In another week when the weather turns warm, it won't be fit for man nor beast out here."

Rebecca wrinkled her nose.

Adam cleared his throat.

A bullfrog croaked, deep and bass, then with a splash he dived from his lily pad.

"Someday," said Adam, with a voice that sounded detached and distant, "I'd like to ask a very special young lady to marry me."

"Why don't you?" Rebecca's voice was as silken as the surface of the moonlit millpond, but her heart, she was sure, beat so loudly that Adam must certainly hear.

"Because . . . because whenever I think of marriage, I think of all its benefits for me, and I feel so selfish, so unworthy."

"I made up my mind years ago that I'd marry only for one reason," replied Rebecca.

Her heart, she was sure, beat so loudly that Adam must certainly hear.

"And what is that?"

"Love."

"I can answer that—I love you!"

"And?"

"Will you marry me?"

"Will you kiss me?"

Adam removed his hat and placed it on the rock beside Rebecca as he turned to face her. She waited until she felt his strong hands slide under her arms and across her back, drawing her close.

Rebecca placed the forefinger of her right hand firmly across Adam's disappointed lips. "Not now, silly. On our wedding day."

15

"AUNT" REBECCA

Aunt Rebecca, please be tyin' my shoe," piped a high child's voice in a lilting Irish brogue. Rebecca hoisted little Patrick O'Rourke onto her lap. Patty's white, almost alabaster complexion made the sad, dark eyes of this waif all the more penetrating. He was light as a feather; though five years old, he seemed to her like a mature two-year-old, this child of New York's city streets.

Rebecca had come to Portland's Maine Home for Little Wayfarers in mid-August to get ready for the inrush of older children, to begin right after Labor Day. But getting ready meant constant interruptions by the two dozen children too small to send to farms who roamed the near-empty dormitories all summer.

Rebecca let her mop handle fall with a clunk against a bunk bed, the mop standing in its bucket of suds. She then wiped Patrick's nose on her own pocket handkerchief. She had considered using the piece of torn bedsheet pinned to Patty's cuff by another matron for the disagreeable task, but she changed her mind when she discovered that, much used and dragged in the dirt, it looked as though the child had been cleaning the coal stove in the parlor with it. She then pulled firmly on the frayed laces of one ankle-length leather shoe, and they snapped in her strong fingers.

"Come on, Patty; let's find you some new laces." He trotted obediently behind her to a supply room where she fished in a drawer until she came up with a small wooden box labeled, "BRN LACES—36 in., 2 DOZ PR." Having found the desired laces, Rebecca passed them to Pat. "Think you can put 'em in yourself?"

"Yes, mum; but I can't tie 'em."

Rebecca checked the watch in her apron pocket. 11:45. "Almost lunchtime, and you need a bath," she said decidedly. "At least we must wash your top half before you may eat. C'mon." Patrick trotted after her to the bathroom, where she sat him on the edge of the tub, a large, soldered, zinc affair encased in an oak box. "You start unlacing your shoes to put the new ones in. I'm washing you up good."

Rebecca found a clean washcloth and a heavy, coarse cotton towel in the bathroom closet, and there was a bar of oatmeal and lye soap on the lavatory. She hastily opened the brass faucet marked "hot," and she found herself splashed before she got it adjusted to a trickle.

A bathroom was a luxury not afforded even at the brick house. In Riverboro, only Watson, the grocer, had a bathroom, and it depended on the feeble flowage of a spring in the side of Guide Board Hill for water pressure. Rebecca had learned to use bathrooms at Wareham Academy, but the plumbing there was fed from an aging wooden reservoir set at roof level, so the water pressure was weak, at best, and nonexistent on the second floor of the girls' dormitory when the downstairs baths were in use.

But Portland had "city" water, with pressure enough, Rebecca was sure, to drive a small locomotive. And so, unless she approached the faucets with greatest caution, she invariably got herself drenched. As for Patty, he seemed not to know what wash water was for, be it city water or country water. For him water evidently served but one purpose—drinking when he had been running or playing; his fascination with the drinking fountain was so thorough, Rebecca discovered, that he had to be restricted in its use.

"Water's cold," Patty complained, as Rebecca commenced to scrub his grimy neck.

"That's because the coal furnace is off until fall. How'd you wash before you came here?" she inquired.

"Mother'd heat it in her teakettle," he said simply.

"What became of your mother?" Rebecca, reluctant as she was to pry into the child's unhappy past, was nonetheless curious about the origins of her new charges.

"She died," he answered matter-of-factly. "They took her away in a hearse with my little sister after two days."

"Did your sister die, too?"

"Yes, mum."

Rebecca stopped scrubbing and began to cry. Quickly drying her tears on the towel, she also dried Patty, rubbing vigorously over one spot which had failed to come clean in the washing. She sat him on her lap and began quickly to replace his broken laces. "I had a sister die, too," Rebecca said.

"Did *your* mother die?"

"No, Patty. My mother is very much alive. She lives in Riverboro, only an hour's ride by train and two hours further by horse and stagecoach."

"You get to ride a stagecoach when you go home? That must be grand! Are there any Injuns in Riverboro?"

"Dear me, no, Patty," Rebecca laughed. "Now let's go to lunch." She set her charge on his feet, and hand in hand "Aunt" Rebecca and her newfound friend trotted off to the dining room.

Rebecca's first two weeks at Wayfarers were spent scrubbing floors and woodwork, waxing what seemed like acres of brown linoleum, washing panes of glass in what she was sure were a hundred double-hung windows, dusting shelves, and beating carpets. Those orphaned urchins, because of immature age, small stature, or other apparent lack of fitness for farm work, had been passed over in the spring by Yankee farmers looking for strong backs and quick hands and were more or less under the supervision of whichever matron happened to be nearest their play area.

Rebecca loved children, but despised she the mop, the scrub brush, and the dust cloth. A broom she could tolerate, for that handy, handled tool could be easily wielded to remove just enough dirt for civilized living, yet required little drudgery and less bending than the other tools of housewifery.

True, under Aunt Miranda's tutelage, Rebecca had become a tolerable housekeeper. And at Aunt Jane's direction, she had accomplished a fair degree of skill with the needle, crochet hook, and sewing machine. But Rebecca's fingers seemed far more fitted for piano keys and quill pens, and her heart was happier in the library than in the laundry.

Even as her departed Aunt Miranda had taught her the sterner, useful disciplines of life, her years as a child at Sunnybrook had bestowed in Rebecca's heart a love for children—clean ones, dirty ones; quiet ones, crying ones; those of sweet demeanor and those of sour disposition. She who was loath to scrub a kitchen floor would happily scour an urchin's face. It was not the removal of dirt which repulsed Rebecca, it was just that what she found under a child's dirt was far more interesting than the maple or oak of a floor.

If washing windows made Rebecca dour, opening the windows of a child's heart with a song, a psalm, or a book of tales delighted her soul and lifted her spirit. Rebecca loved children; loved them with all her heart, with all her soul, and with all her mind—though she confessed there was a mystery in this, in that she loved God with all her being as well and loved Adam Ladd fully also. Her relationship with the charges given into her hand was an affair of the heart: she could not help but love them, and her intellect was incapable of unraveling this dilemma.

Not all the dwellers on Munjoy Hill, however, shared Rebecca's affection for the orphans. Munjoy Hill was an enclave of the homes of Portland's first citizens, and not a few resented having this island of mercy within their midst. The Wayfarers' complex consisted of a sprawling four-story mansard-roof mansion, its guest house, stables, and carriage house on two acres of the best residential property in the neighborhood. It had been left to charity by old Samuel Saltonstall, whose mother had died at his birth and whose father had died months earlier.

Mr. Saltonstall had had no children to inherit his property; he had, however, raised ten orphans in his mansion with the help of his good wife and their entourage of servants. Each of these children he had given ten thousand dollars from his fortune in the shipping business, and he had rewarded each of his servants amply upon their retirement, as well. The children had been sent out into the world like Hagar's Ishmael when each reached his majority at twenty-one, and he had instructed them to use their inheritances wisely in seeking their own fortunes in the world. Five had become substantial citizens with the aid of their share of Saltonstall's cash; two had lost theirs in unwise ventures, then, wiser, had built businesses on their experience. Three had reduced themselves to poverty, and it looked unlikely that they would recover. "Two evils have I seen under the sun," old Sam Saltonstall was wont to say, "the miser who leaves his riches for his relatives to fight over and the heir who lives in want until his children are grown and then inherits wealth and dies rich."

So, with his bank account dispersed among those who became his children while they were still young enough to enjoy it, old Saltonstall moved in with an adopted daughter's family and put his estate into a foundation, of which Miss Edythe Leonard was made the prudent and wise president. This was ten years since, and Saltonstall had meanwhile gone to his own reward.

Miss Leonard, sharp businesswoman that she was, saw no need for either horses or carriages at the Wayfarers' Home, for the streetcars ran right past the front gate. So a carpenter was employed and the carriage house and stable were refurbished into classrooms for instruction in such practical arts as home economics and woodworking. In the space between the buildings, swings, slides, a teeter-totter, and a trapeze were installed for the entertainment of the younger children. Mr. Saltonstall's tennis courts and Mrs. Saltonstall's flower beds were removed; for, though Miss Leonard dearly loved flowers, she loved children even more dearly.

A ball diamond was laid out where the courts and gardens had been. In the elms along the estate's back yard brick walls, Miss Leonard ordered that chicken wire netting be strung to prevent home-run hits from landing in neighbors' yards. But the netting, rather than placating the wrath of the prejudiced, riled the neighbors so much that some would have run Miss Leonard's brood into the hinterlands out of spite. And when an errant fly ball did manage to pass above the wire netting, the ire of certain neighbors was sure to be raised.

Rebecca, who in the course of growing up had learned nearly every game known to children of either sex, was, as soon as the older youngsters returned from their summer labors, drafted captain of whichever afternoon ball team she chose. "Aunt Rebecca's *our* captain," rival sides would cry in unison. Rebecca decided which team to head by the flip of a coin—until the coin fell the same way three days in a row; from then on she settled on being captain of each team on alternate days.

It was Rebecca's turn at bat on the second day of her new big-league experience. Her team was ahead five to three in the bottom of the fourth of a five-inning game, and giddy with more fame than Casey, yet not wishing to be accused of unfair competition, she had taken two wild swings at the opposing pitcher's fastball. Brooklyn Pete, a barefoot boy of fourteen, was the pitcher, and as he squinted under the brim of his ragged felt hat, a wicked gleam in his eye seemed to say, "I'm going to get you on this one."

Rebecca pounded the plate and twirled her bat in purposeful defiance.

Pete wound up, spitting in the dirt between missing teeth, as he raised his left foot to sight across the plate between his toes. The ball hissed wickedly through the air.

Rebecca swung, too low for a hit. She tipped the ball off the end of her bat, and it arched up, up and out in a high, far-right-field foul. The ball went over the wire fence, disappearing among some mulberry bushes on the edge of Mr. Eustis MacGregor's cucumber patch behind his horse stable.

"There goes our last ball," groaned Pete.

"Yeah," said another. "Ol' MacGregor'll kill us for sure if we go git it."

"He'll be over here to bawl out Miss Leonard anyway," said a third.

"*She'll* tell old man MacGregor where to get off, like she did before," another said.

"I'll go get it," Rebecca volunteered pleasantly, not as yet fully appreciative of the terrors of Mr. MacGregor's cucumber patch. She had retrieved many a ball as a child, not a few of which she herself had knocked over fences. Her feet were bare like the children's, since she preferred not to scuff her new leather shoes in a game of sandlot ball. So, hiking her skirts up to her shins, she ran out the gate and around the corner.

The gate to the MacGregor yard was open wide, and Rebecca trotted up the long walk toward the house, at the same time craning her neck to see if she could spy the children's ball. She mounted the steps of the imposing brownstone mansion and twirled the brass handle on the mechanical bell. Getting no response, she surveyed the garden from the vantage point of the porch. Sure enough, there was the ball, on the strip of grass between a mulberry tree and the cucumber patch.

In Riverboro one seldom asks a neighbor's permission to retrieve a ball or a kite or a stray sheep or a calf. One merely does it, and nobody minds. If there were damage, it would certainly be repaired or paid for; but to ask permission to retrieve one's own property which had accidently landed in another's yard is ordinarily considered an affront. So though the orphan's warnings had made her nervous, Rebecca now carefully skirted the cucumber bed, taking care not to tread on any errant vines spread on the grass. She picked up the ball, dropped it in her apron pocket, and turned to leave.

"Reach for the sky, you unwashed female orphan," came an angry, rasping male voice behind her. "Try to run, you ratty whelp, and I'll plug you through."

Rebecca turned slowly to meet old Eustis MacGregor's red face. He had been in his stable grooming his driving horses and had not heard his doorbell. Rebecca did not raise her hands, but she made a point of keeping them in sight. She gingerly walked toward the scowling, balding man of about sixty, who was pointing a double-barreled shotgun directly at her chest, keeping her eyes fixed on his as she moved. *Scrunch!* a yellow, ripe cucumber squashed beneath one bare foot. She moved away and succeeded only in stepping on a second one. "As you can see, I'm not armed, sir," she said. "Don't you think you'd better point that gun the other direction before somebody gets hurt?"

"It's not loaded," he glumly admitted, lowering his twelve-gauge.

"In that case, you can hit me with it if I attack you, sir. I'm Rebecca Randall."

"Gimme whatcha got in yer pocket."

"I have a watch in my pocket, a handkerchief, a pencil, a piece of chalk, and a ball. Which one do you want?"

"Don't get smart with me. You New York kids are all alike—you think you can rob a man, then sass him like you haven't done anything! You stepped on two of my ripe pickling cukes, and you picked something up from under my tree!"

"I'm not from New York; I've never been out of Maine in my life, as a matter of fact, sir. But what's in my pocket is *my* property, and I think you're rude to demand it, though I do apologize for squashing your cucumbers."

"This is my yard, and those are my cukes!"

"Granted. And I'll be happy to pay for them, though I'm sure you took two cucumbers' worth of life out of me when you scared me with your silly shooting iron. But those are my kids," she continued, motioning toward several juvenile faces peeping over the wall. "I agreed to get their ball back for them. I'm the new matron and girls' housemother, and I had hoped to have a pleasant chat with each of our neighbors some day soon." With that, she fished out the ball, held it up for Mr. MacGregor's cursory inspection, then she hurled it high over the chicken wire toward Pete, who was waiting in slack-jawed admiration of Rebecca's bravery from the other side. "Game's over," she shouted at the children. "Back to your duties, now." Turning to Mr. MacGregor, she inquired, "Do you have a moment? I'd like to chat with you."

Rebecca shortly convinced Mr. MacGregor that she was really a nice enough person, though he remained skeptical about the orphanage. "Orphanages ought to be out in the country," he grumbled, "so's the kids can roam. Nice neighborhoods with fenced yards are no place for children. Besides, they spend their summers working on farms, and then they come back too wild for city life, with less manners than when they came here from New York or Boston or Hartford in the first place."

"I agree with you; the country *is* the best place to raise children," was Rebecca's pleasant reply. "But Mr. Saltonstall left the Wayfarers a home in the *city,* so I guess we'll just have to stay here and make the best of it."

"You could sell and move. Those kids need a year-round home where they don't have to be uprooted twice yearly. I have children myself, and grandchildren, and I can tell you it's not right."

"And could I meet Mrs. MacGregor?"

"My wife departed this life two years ago," he said with sorrow in his voice.

"I'm sorry." Rebecca patted his hand. "Do you see your grandchildren often?"

"My family is scattered all over New England, so I see them twice a year, at most."

"Perhaps we can fix you up with some grandchildren on a more regular basis," Rebecca offered merrily as she rose to leave.

❧ ❧ ❧

Two days later Rebecca was back visiting Mr. MacGregor, this time with an apple pie she had baked in the Wayfarers' kitchen. This time he entertained her and Maxine, a fourteen-year-old motherless Boston girl, on his glassed-in back porch. MacGregor, who had retired after years in the shipbuilding business, was proud of his cucumber garden and the varieties of excellent pickles he had succeeded in making from them. There were sweet gherkins from the early crop; sweet chunk pickles from the ripe cucumbers of late summer; brined dill pickles, both sliced and whole; chunk green pickles with onions; and cucumber relish. These he brought out on a tray and let Rebecca and Maxine sample each in turn. Pie and pickles, accompanied by cheese and hot tea supplied by Mr. MacGregor, made a delightful afternoon treat indeed.

"Come back again, girls," he warmly remarked as they were leaving. "And Miss Randall," he added, "please accept my humble apologies for the fright with the shotgun. I've lived here many years, and I guess I feel persecuted and hemmed in by so many noisy youngsters."

"Perhaps we can help each other," Rebecca laughed lightly as they took their leave.

❧ ❧ ❧

"That's what impressed me about you when you came here for an interview last winter, Rebecca—your rapport with people," remarked Miss Leonard, as days later in her office, Rebecca related her experience with Mr. MacGregor. Edythe Leonard adjusted her pince-nez on her nose, then dipped her head and looked over her eyeglasses at Rebecca. "Please be seated."

Rebecca took her seat in a leather-cushioned oak chair before the desk and sat up, prim and alert. "Yes, Miss Leonard?"

"Our neighbors, as I'm sure you know by now, have been less than supportive of our program at Wayfarers."

"I gathered as much."

"In the decade we've been here, your overture is the first effective reconciliation that's been made—the first bridge that's been built."

"But why is there so much animosity?" Rebecca asked. "Our children are well mannered; the grounds are well kept. Mr. MacGregor says there hasn't been a single incident of vandalism from our students."

"The usual excuse is that we're hurting neighborhood property values, while as a non-profit organization we don't pay taxes. The late Mrs. MacGregor was furious when we took out the flower beds and tennis courts. It seems that the MacGregors and the Saltonstalls used to play tennis together every summer weekend. She went straight to city hall to complain that we were destroying valuable residential property and hurting the neighborhood."

"But we're *not* hurting the neighborhood!" Rebecca protested. "Children are an asset. This stodgy old hill needs a few *real* children to liven it up. Why, in five blocks walking to the market yesterday I saw just one child—a curly headed kid in blue knickers and *white* stockings. His sailor cap was hitched to his collar with a cord. I'll bet his mama'd spank him if he so much as soiled a sock chasing his cap!"

"Then there are those who believe the place for an orphanage is out in the country, surrounded by fields and forests." Miss Leonard sighed deeply. "But we were given a city estate, not a farm," she added in indignation.

"I think some folks resent having the poor, the orphaned, or the maimed around," Rebecca observed. "It reminds them of their own frailty, I'm afraid. As for a country location, it seems to me that that *would* be ideal. But as you say, we can't just uproot these buildings and grounds and transplant them to the countryside."

"You're a very perceptive young lady. And I have no trouble agreeing that country living would be ideal, if it were possible!"

"If I am blessed with any perception, I owe it to my own growing-up days as a half-orphan living with maiden aunts of independent means—not wealthy, but we had far more at the brick house in Riverboro than at Sunnybrook Farm in Temperance."

"There's a vast difference between never quite enough and just enough," agreed Miss Leonard.

"Neither poverty nor riches, that we may always remember who is the Giver of every good and perfect gift," added Rebecca earnestly.

"Rebecca, our board of directors has asked me to appoint an assistant director. This person will take full responsibility of affairs when I am absent and will have authority over the other help as it becomes necessary."

Rebecca shifted uncomfortably in her chair. She had worked for Miss Leonard just over a month, and she had grown very fond of her. From the outset Edythe Leonard, though nearly old enough to be Rebecca's mother, had entrusted her with responsibility and had even instructed several of the day help to answer to Rebecca, releasing her so that she could attend to correspondence and business administration. Now, apparently, Miss Leonard was about to hire an assistant. And Rebecca's limited experience had taught her that straw bosses could be arrogant and abusive.

"Will you be my assistant, Rebecca?"

"Miss Leonard, I'll be happy . . . excuse me—what did you just ask me?" Rebecca blurted out.

"I need an assistant. You are the only one here besides myself with an academy education. And already you have won the respect of the entire institution."

"Do . . . do you *really* think I can do it?"

"I've watched people grow into jobs for years," said Miss Leonard. "Too many managerial positions are filled by pedantic drudges who reached the level of their incompetence long before they were promoted. There are the Hamans who seek position merely because they crave the prominence. On the other hand, there are the Josephs, who, though content to be a responsible slave, soon find themselves second only to Pharaoh and doing the king's business well. You have the makings of a Joseph, if you will let the Lord use you, Rebecca."

"Then I accept your offer," Rebecca answered quietly. "And if you'll agree, I'd like to launch a new program which I believe will create goodwill among our neighbors, as well as be of great benefit to our children," she suggested boldly.

❧ ❧ ❧

In the weeks that followed, Rebecca, sometimes accompanied by Maxine, sometimes by Brooklyn Pete or another orphan who might be any age from five to fourteen, visited every single Munjoy Hill home, walking several blocks in every direction. By late October she had laid the groundwork of her plan.

"Hi, I'm Rebecca Randall, the new assistant headmistress at the Wayfarers' Home," Rebecca would announce at each door. "This is Maxine, from Boston, and she is our guest here in Maine. Her parents died right after they came to America. May we step inside and tell you about a new program we are undertaking at Wayfarers?"

Almost invariably, Rebecca and the orphan gained entrance. Even those most opposed to an orphanage in the neighborhood wanted to learn what this "new program" was in order to better resist it.

"Tell me, what do *you* see for the future of Wayfarers' Home?" Rebecca would often inquire of each householder. Answers ranged from embarrassed stammers to angry denunciations of the orphans who had the "audacity to set themselves up in a fine city neighborhood." Many comments, however, were positive and constructive. Rebecca hoped to disarm hostility by giving folks a chance to air their feelings and their fears about the Home for Wayfarers.

Rebecca's program was simplicity itself: She needed surrogate grandparents for the Wayfarers' residents. They would remember their surrogate grandchild on his or her birthday, Thanksgiving, Christmas, and Easter; invite this child to their home for occasional weekends and holidays; and, at least, send an occasional gift and visit the orphanage for the Christmas cantata and Easter pageant.

Rebecca had asked Miss Leonard for money to have a flier printed explaining the responsibilities of grandparents, and to hire a photographer, so that each grandparent might have a small photo of his "grandchild." The budget for this publicity, ten dollars, was two weeks' salary for Rebecca, a fact which Miss Leonard pointed out when she turned down Rebecca's request.

Rebecca didn't sleep that night until she promised the Lord that, if He didn't supply the money by other means, she'd take it out of her savings. Next morning she found herself behind Miss Leonard's desk to answer the phone and some correspondence while the headmistress was downtown on business.

"Citizens Complain to City Council About Orphanage on Hill," the headline read on a yellowed *Press-Herald* clipping tucked into a corner of Miss Leonard's desk blotter. Rebecca frowned on reading the headline, then turned the article over without reading it. She wanted only happy thoughts to pass her mind this morning.

Then a happy thought struck. Rebecca turned the clipping face up again and read the reporter's name, a Miss Nellie Bagley. Rebecca phoned the *Press-Herald,* got Miss Bagley on the line, and very quickly struck a deal. The Wayfarers' Home would open its doors for a reporter to do a feature story on the orphanage's work with the children of immigrants. The *Press-Herald* would send its photographer to accompany Miss Bagley, and as a courtesy to Rebecca, the newspaper would furnish her photographs of all the children and one hundred copies of a printed flier she herself would write.

Edythe Leonard at first expressed shock, then apprehension, then finally, an acceptance of Rebecca's presumptuous arrangements with the *Press-Herald.* "The publicity will either ruin us or revive us, and who can tell which," Miss Leonard concluded. "I suppose the matter ought to be taken to the board of directors first."

"Boards are committees, and the usual function of committees is to kill good ideas," Rebecca answered tartly.

Miss Leonard, however, took no offense at Rebecca's indignation. Instead, with a twinkle in her serious gray eyes, she responded, "You know, you're right. I admire your decisiveness and spunk, Rebecca. We shall go ahead with your arrangements and see what happens."

Rebecca's program to gain support from the Munjoy Hill community received mixed reviews. About a dozen—not nearly enough—caring citizens took orphans into their homes for birthdays and holidays. Perhaps three times as many came to the thirty-voice Christmas cantata which, under Rebecca's direction, had practiced twice weekly for a month. This turned the attitude of the community at large in favor of the Wayfarers and gave the children a real feeling of accomplishment.

Maxine and several other older orphaned girls Rebecca placed as part-time companions and helpers in the homes of several elderly, going once or twice weekly to help with the laundry and cleaning or to read aloud the letters from relatives to those whose eyes were dim with age. Mr. MacGregor employed Maxine each Saturday, and he hired Brooklyn Pete to rake his yard and help tend his horses. This employment gave these homeless a sense of achievement, which would aid them in becoming independent and self-sufficient adults.

Mr. MacGregor also became the Wayfarers' benefactor, not only in delivering great crocks of delicious cucumber pickles for their daily table, but in cash donations to meet special needs. Too, Mr. MacGregor's vocal support turned the attitude of many neighbors in favor of Wayfarers.

But Rebecca, as much as she loved her work, was troubled whenever she remembered Mr. MacGregor's remark that the children needed a "year-round home where they don't have to be uprooted twice yearly." Would she someday be able to help provide waifs such as these from city streets with suitable surroundings, where they could develop their hearts, minds, and bodies outside the stifling confines of a musty old stone mansion, she often pondered.

16

AUNT SARAH'S RELEASE

Adam Ladd was the one familiar face from Rebecca's childhood she was privileged to see during the Christmas holidays. Adam, whom Rebecca viewed as the link to her future as well as a tie to her past, reserved for Christmas Eve and Day a room in Portland's Eastland Hotel, which he often used on business trips for the Boston & Down East Railway Company.

Rebecca must stay at Wayfarers' Home over Christmas. For nearly a hundred orphans, this was their only home, except from May through September when they were let out to work on farms—to pick peas and apples, to pitch hay, to pick up potatoes, to rake blueberries. "Aunt" Rebecca was for many of these children their only mother. She was the one who wiped their noses and dried their tears, who untangled and tied their laces, nursed their barked knees and skinned elbows, combed their hair; she rubbed their croupy chests with camphorated oil, tied their ribbons and bows, lined them up to measure their growth; and she demonstrated how to press a slippery piece of codfish onto a barbed hook during a Saturday excursion mackerel fishing off the long pier in Portland harbor.

For these youngsters, Rebecca was Santa Claus and much more. To them, Rebecca became, not the Christ of the Bible, surely, but His undershepherd. She would point their untutored hearts to the true Christ whom they could not see.

So Christmas Eve found Rebecca cross-legged beneath the Christmas tree with three dozen girls gathered around on rugs and cushions as she read the Christmas story, which told of the Gift greater than those brought by the Magi. "There's a gentleman at the door, Aunt Rebecca," interrupted a girl who had gone to answer the insistent clanging of the brass gong in the front entry. "He says he wants to see you."

"Please bring him in, by all means," Rebecca answered merrily. "He may sit quietly in the back row 'til I am finished with the Christmas story, and then I'll introduce him."

It was Adam, and he took a seat at the invitation of a skinny child of eleven, red-haired Ruby, who hopped onto the rug and sat with the others, enraptured with Rebecca's animated storytelling. The Bible came alive—the children *saw* the angels hovering above the humble manger in the Judean cavern; they *heard* the heavenly voices chanting peace on earth to men of goodwill.

"The kids'll be in bed right away, Adam," Rebecca explained, as soon as the Christmas story was done and she had introduced him as her "very special friend." "I got your note that you were coming, so I called on Mrs. Wood, one of our widowed volunteer grandmothers, to stay with the girls until midnight, when my chariot changes back into a pumpkin," she teased.

"Take your time, by all means. I'll wait here by the fireplace," he answered genially.

❧ ❧ ❧

The white gleam of gas lamps cast eerie shadows across Portland's cobbled streets as, arm in arm, Rebecca and Adam strolled through the night. The sky had been overcast all day; now it was snowing, and white flakes slid sideways in the salt sea air of this coastal city, peppering the granite curbs and paving stones. The couple walked on in silence, savoring each other's company, or speaking in fragments of thoughts spun off by their months of letter writing.

"I love these children," Rebecca said at last. "I have a ministry here, and yet I feel these youngsters are being shortchanged somehow. There are so many well-to-do people right here in Portland, and there must be thousands more across our nation who could do so much more," she said earnestly.

"I'm a railroad man," answered Adam. "I've seen success, but now I'd like to leave this business and move into something more directly involved with the needs of people," he said. "You've probably guessed that it was I who put your name in the hopper for your position here as a housemother and matron—so you see, like yourself, I have an interest in orphanages."

"Assistant headmistress," Rebecca corrected Adam.

"What about the assistant headmistress?" Adam was puzzled.

"I was promoted in October—I've been saving it to surprise you."

"You don't say! I guess that means you'll be staying here a few years." His voice showed surprise, then restrained disappointment.

"I don't think so, Adam. I'd much prefer to work at a home where the children stay year-round, like a normal home. Preferably it should be a country environment. Perhaps someday, the brick house. . . ."

"But the brick house has got to be home for your mother and the girls and Aunt Jane for several years yet," he interrupted.

"But still, I can dream."

"I like your dreams," said Adam. "Not only do you dream, but you have a way of making those dreams come true."

"The old see visions of the hereafter; the young, those young who *can* dream, dream dreams of after the here and now," Rebecca said lightly but with a sagacity which startled Adam. "But it is God who fulfills both our visions and our dreams," she added.

The couple strolled on, until at last the snow began to dim the hissing gas streetlights and decorate the barren elms and maples with frozen frosting. Dully in the distance a church tower clock began to toll. They stopped and counted: eleven bass strokes reverberated in the darkness. "That's the clock on First Church; it's downtown," Rebecca remarked.

"I know that landmark," acknowledged Adam. "The question is, which way did the sound come from—I can't tell in the storm—and which way is back to the Wayfarers' Home?"

"Frankly, I'm lost," Rebecca admitted. "We've been out—oh, my, nearly two hours, and I promised Mrs. Wood I'd be back so she could go home at twelve. If we were to go straight back, we still couldn't make it on time. And the streetcars don't run after ten o'clock."

"In Boston they run all night, but I'm afraid a Boston trolley wouldn't help much here in Portland," Adam commented. "But there's still a way out of this. I can't promise to have you back by midnight, but I shall try. So come on."

Adam turned down a side street that pitched steeply downhill.

"Where are we going?"

"Downtown—the waterfront business district. As long as we're moving downhill, we'll end up at the harbor. From there it'll be a simple matter to find my hotel, and I can phone for a cab from the lobby."

Just as the church clock tolled eleven-thirty, Rebecca and Adam at last walked out of the residential district into a commercial area strange to both of them. Stretching for blocks were glass-front stores and quaint little shops with street-level, multi-paned windows. Except for a feeble kerosene or gas light in an upstairs apartment window here and there, and the flicker of the gas streetlights, all was dark. "The Eastland Hotel is at least a dozen blocks yet, clear to the other side of this district, I'm sure," said Adam. He pointed to a gap in the buildings, where they could see a wharf, looming black over the water. "If we keep the water to our left, we'll be going south along the harbor. I thought we'd reach the shore further south and nearer the hotel," he said with anxiety in his voice.

Two blocks down, a door opened and two laughing men and a woman emerged. The laughter faded as the trio shuffled off into the night.

"Wait!" Adam whispered. The door opened again, and a man left as another entered. "A tavern, I think. Not the most wholesome establishment, but they may have a telephone."

"*I'm* not going in with you!"

"It was just an idea," Adam answered. "What's this?" He stepped into the gutter by the curb and picked up a stout stick of machine-turned wood.

As he held the stick up to a street lamp, Rebecca could see that it was a broken carriage wheel spoke. "What are you going to do with that?" she inquired nervously.

"Don't ask." He whacked the snow off on a curb stone and crammed it into his overcoat pocket. "Just cross the street with me, if you please." Adam was still acting the gentleman, but he was growing tense and nervous. Cautiously he picked his way along the sidewalk until they were opposite the tavern, not passing a set-in doorway or an alley without looking in searchingly as they stepped by, Adam often checking back over his shoulder. Adam chose a dark doorway opposite the tavern where he and Rebecca huddled together. Was it growing colder, or was the blood cooling in their veins, they both wondered together.

"How long shall we wait?" Rebecca inquired earnestly.

Adam pulled out his watch, then he struck a match. 11:43. "Any moment, now," he said.

The "clip-clop, clip-clop" of a trotting horse startled Rebecca. "C'mon," cried Adam, stepping into the street as he led her by the arm. "Taxi—cab!"

The driver of the hansom stopped his horse in the middle of the street, the beast panting and steaming in the eerie gaslight. The hack driver stared at the couple running from the doorway.

"Do you have a fare?" Adam asked.

"Nosuh, 'less you're it."

"Good! I need you for about an hour."

"Cash up front, mistuh. Two dollars this time o' night!"

Adam produced a two-dollar bill. "Know where Wayfarers' Home is?"

"That the off'nidge on Munjoy Hill? Have you there'n ten minutes." He swung the door wide and held it for Rebecca to enter.

"Good. Can you take a lady home afterward, then take me to the Eastland Hotel, or does your horse have that much wind left in him?"

"My hoss'll go ennywheres, so's I gets paid an' he gets fed."

"Get us there safely, my man, and I'll match that two-dollar bill with another for Christmas." With that, Adam hopped in after Rebecca, and the driver slammed the door.

"How'd you know there'd be a taxi along this time of night?" Rebecca asked as the light carriage jounced over the cobblestones.

"Simple. The bartender has to close up shop at midnight on Christmas Eve. I figured that a late-working hack driver or two would be along just before midnight to pick up some last-minute change from the revelers. But we beat 'em to it."

"Clever. But why the cudgel?" Rebecca patted the pocket in which Adam had deposited his stick.

"Oh, that? Here." He fished it out and passed it to her. "Toss it in the fireplace on your way to bed. We're home!"

"But . . . but, why did you pick it up?"

Adam grinned sheepishly. "A wise man never goes into a waterfront district at midnight without a proper weapon," he explained. "The clock's striking now. You'd better go get Mrs. Wood." He helped her down, and with an "I'll be right out, cabbie" to the driver, Adam walked Rebecca to the door. "What time do you eat Christmas dinner?"

"What makes you think you're invited?" Rebecca teased.

"You wrote me last week, remember?"

She patted his cheek. "G'night. I'll send Mrs. Wood right down."

❧ ❧ ❧

Adam proved to be the life of the party for the children after Christmas dinner. Not only did the youngsters love him at once, as he took the smaller ones on his knee and told Christmas stories from his own childhood, but he himself seemed totally at ease among them.

"When will I see you again, Adam?" Rebecca said, when finally the last youngster had been tucked in and they were alone by the fire in the old mansion's guest parlor.

"February—around Valentine's Day. I'll rent a room at the Eastland, and if you can get a few hours free we can go out to eat."

Tears started in Rebecca's eyes as Adam spoke. "I understand darling," he said tenderly. "Valentine's Day brings back painful memories for both of us."

She dabbed her tears with her handkerchief and looked him full in the face, then she patted his cheek. "Don't think of it. He who said 'I am the resurrection' also said 'I am the life.' We have a life to live, and we can be happy on Valentine's Day. But we must make some plans, and I think February's a good time to start making some 'to do' lists."

Adam smiled happily. "To do is fine. But first, *when*—we've got to set a date."

"My year here is up in mid-August, but I'm not coming back, even if we did not marry. Most of my charges leave for the farms by the middle of May; so I expect under the circumstances Miss Leonard will let me go at the end of May with little fuss. How does the third Saturday in June sound for a wedding, if I can arrange it? If I have to wait a single minute once preparations are finished, I'll lose my mind of excitement."

"I'm going to lose mine anyway," Adam joked. "But June is fine. The work on the new Sunnybrook Depot is to be substantially done by then, and I can take some time off."

"So you're going to North Riverboro on the train tomorrow morning? When're you heading back to Boston?"

"Within two or three days. By the weekend, at the latest."

"Please do me a special favor while at your Aunt Mary's," Rebecca asked. "Aunt Sarah Cobb, a very dear friend of mine, has not been well since Thanksgiving, Mother writes. It'll be three weeks, yet, before I go home in mid-January, when John has his semester break from Bowdoin. Please look in on her and give her my love."

"I know the Cobbs, of course," said Adam. "Aunt Sarah is the telephone operator, isn't she?"

"Yes. But Jenny had been tending the switchboard for her while she's been down. Mother wrote to say that Aunt Sarah is on her feet much of the time; but constantly running to plug up people's party lines is wearing her down. So Jenny's making herself a little cash for shoes and school supplies for when she starts classes at Wareham next month. The telephone company doesn't pay much, but it's time Jenny learned some responsibility besides housework."

"I seem to remember that you were quite an accomplished businesswoman at thirteen," Adam laughed. He paused as the old Seth Thomas mantel clock above the fireplace counted out eleven chimes. "It's late. I've got a long day tomorrow. May I use the phone to call a cab?"

Rebecca stood long on the door stoop as the hansom carrying Adam to his hotel jounced off down the street, the muffled clatter of the horse's hooves on the new-fallen snow fading in the distance. The hackney horse turned the corner under a street lamp, and she caught the gleam of the steam from the animal's nostrils as it disappeared from view.

Rebecca returned to her duties in the girls' dorm wing of the old house. One child needed a hot water bottle for a tummy ache. Red-haired Ruby, who often cried herself to sleep, was having nightmares, and Rebecca sat on the edge of the child's bed with a comforting hand on her back, singing softly, until at last Ruby was breathing deeply again. The clock struck midnight as Rebecca slipped into her own bed and slid silently beneath her covers.

Rebecca dreamed that night, dreams unlike the dreams of many nights previous, in which she had dreamed of the faces of orphaned, motherless children, faces sad or merry, faces with eyes searching for her eyes. She dreamed instead of a black hansom drawn by a chestnut mare fading into the still, cold night. That cab carried the man of her dreams. Would he, like the cab that carried him, fade from her vision; or would Adam Ladd grow in her view and fulfill her dreams of the future?

❧ ❧ ❧

Rebecca's train pulled into Maplewood Depot moments after the Riverboro stagecoach had disappeared over the hill. The train had been delayed by a shifting freight in Gorham, and it was half an hour behind schedule. Rebecca considered renting a one-horse buggy, but she had five days in Riverboro. Then she planned to take the narrow gauge into Wareham to visit sister Jenny and Emily Maxwell before going from there back to Portland by the indirect route. So to rent a rig would require a trip back to Maplewood tomorrow, and half a day wasted.

"May I use the phone to call Riverboro? I'm stranded and I need a ride," she asked the depot master.

"Ayuh. Costs a nickel," he glumly muttered, "an' reverse the charges fer toll calls." Rebecca paid him, and he jerked his thumb at a wall phone behind his counter.

"Riverboro, one-one, ring one-three," Rebecca told the Maplewood operator.

"Riverboro central. Numbuh please," came the crisp answer a moment later.

"Line eleven, ring thirteen," the Maplewood operator answered.

"Excuse me," Rebecca cut in, "may I speak to the Riverboro operator?"

"It's a little unusual," protested Maplewood central.

"Becky!" Riverboro central cried. Then, "It's all right, Maplewood operator. It's my daughter. I'll speak to her."

"But we've *got* to charge you for a toll call," protested Maplewood. "Company policy."

"Charge it to one-one, ring one-three; that's my number," Rebecca protested.

"I'll have to call through and get their permission," Maplewood insisted. "Whose name is the phone in?"

"Miranda Sawyer," Rebecca answered.

"Are you Miranda Sawyer?"

"No, operator."

"Then I'll have to speak to Miranda Sawyer and get her permission to charge your toll call to the Riverboro operator to her line, eleven ring thirteen." Maplewood central had put on her most official voice for this declaration.

"You can't do that!" Rebecca answered, a bit sharply at this point.

"Why can't I?"

"Maplewood, this is Riverboro," Aurelia interrupted. "My daughter is right. You can't reach Miranda Sawyer because she has been dead nearly two years. But I think I can accept the responsibility for charging a toll call to her phone, since I am her sister and I live at her former residence. The Saco River Telephone Company hasn't objected to toll calls to that number so far, so long as we pay the phone bill."

"Well, I nevuh . . . but go ahead; we've tied the trunk line up too long already." Maplewood central seemed unconvinced, but she had clearly given up the quarrel.

"Mother, why are you tending central?" Rebecca asked at last.

"Sarah Cobb passed away suddenly in the night yesterday; with Jenny away at Wareham Academy, Jane and I are tending the switchboard until it can be moved over to Watson's store. Mrs. Watson and Persis will be the new operators."

"I knew . . . I knew Aunt Sarah was ill, but I didn't know she was gravely ill," Rebecca responded, shocked.

"Yes, my dear. Her funeral is tomorrow. I'll tell you the rest when you get home. Where are you calling from, Becky?'"

"Maplewood Depot. I missed the stage."

"I'll call John. He got in from Bowdoin College yesterday. He'll be after you soon's he kin git Dick-Boy harnessed up."

❧ ❧ ❧

"Sarah Cobb had an inoperable tumor," Aunt Jane explained to Rebecca that evening at the brick house. "She didn't even tell Jeremiah how bad off she was, though the doctor says she had known for some time she could not expect to live and was in a good deal o' pain. She even stayed at the telephone switchboard several hours a day until the day before she died."

"How is Uncle Jerry? How's he taking it?"

"He's beside himself with grief," Jane Sawyer answered her niece. "I've never seen a man suffer so, not even your grandfather when your grandmother died and left him alone. His sister's there, an' she'll be stayin' a couple o' weeks. Course your mother's over tendin' the switchboard; she and I have been takin' turns, but that ends tonight. The phones will be down for about a week while they're movin' the equipment," Jane said.

"I'm going to see Uncle Jerry right now," declared Rebecca, who had not so much as removed her coat. She paused at the door, her hand on the knob. "Don't hold supper for me. If I'm hungry when I get back, I'll fix myself something."

Rebecca found Uncle Jerry in his old rocker beside the kitchen stove, shaking down the coals in the ash pit with a poker as she softly entered. Mindful of his grief, she entered his kitchen through the dark shed without knocking, and slipping across the room, picked up the very same footstool on which she had sat that angry night long ago when she had fled Aunt Miranda's wrath. Carefully she placed the stool by the rocker and sat down. Rebecca waited, one soft hand on the knee of his rough old gabardine pants, until he ceased poking the ashes and dropped the poker into its hole in the corner of the stove.

Jeremiah Cobb apparently took no notice of her, and when softly she murmured, "Uncle Jerry—it's Rebecca," he gazed at her for a moment through tear-swollen eyes, then stared blankly at the wall across the room. Rebecca rested her cheek on the old man's knee, letting her raven tresses fall to the floor across his slippered foot, waiting as she watched the glow of the coals through the stove's open draft. Rebecca's nose told her that a pot of beans was baking in the oven, and it occurred to her that they needed stirring, but she thought better of it.

The ticking of the mantel clock, the crackle of the fire, and the singing of the teakettle in Uncle Jerry's kitchen produced a monotony that Rebecca imagined to be the slow passage of time itself. The only other interruption, besides Uncle Jerry's sighing and breathing, was the occasional buzz from the telephone switchboard in a small room down the hall, and Aurelia's distant, "Central; numbuh please," muffled by the two closed doors between them.

Presently Uncle Jerry patted her head. "Who . . . who is it?" he murmured.

"It's me, your Rebecca."

"Becky, it's you, is it lovey? You've come at a hard time for old Uncle Jerry, a hard time indeed. Did Aurelia send for you?"

"No, Uncle Jerry. I'm sure the Lord sent for me. Here we are with a January thaw setting in, sunny skies every day, and temperatures in the forties. I just said to myself, 'John will be home from college, and I didn't get to see him or the rest of my family or the Cobbs at Christmas.' Mrs. Wood—that's one of our volunteer helpers—was fairly begging for an opportunity to spend a few nights in the girls' dorm at Wayfarers. And Miss Leonard said, 'Rebecca, why don't you take a few days off and go see your family.' I'm sure God knew I needed to be here, and exactly when."

"You mean you . . . you didn't get your mother's letter, the one she said she mailed yesterday?"

"Goodness, no, Uncle Jerry. If Mother mailed a letter yesterday, I couldn't possibly have got it before today, and I was on my way to Riverboro before the mail delivery! Why, what was she planning to tell me?"

"That . . . that your Aunt Sarah died an' went to be with the Lord in the night. She woke me up in the night, an' 'Jerry, I love you,' that's all she said. Them's the very last words I ever heered her say. An' by the time I got a lamp lit, she'd stopped breathin'." Here he began to sob aloud. Rebecca stood up, and with her arms about him, pulled his head to her breast and patted his cheek.

The door from the shed opened, then shut with a bang. A tall, angular woman of perhaps seventy shuffled in, bearing a lighted lantern in one hand and several sticks of stovewood cradled in the crook of one arm. Dropping her wood with a rumble in the woodbox behind Uncle Jerry's rocker, she strode to the kitchen table and set down her lantern. Rebecca watched in silence as the old woman lifted the chimney from the lamp on the kitchen table. She lit and adjusted the wick, then, grasping the chimney with a potholder, replaced it and screwed it in place. She adjusted the wick again, filling the room with a glow as brilliant as the gas lamps in Portland.

"That's a new Aladdin lamp, isn't it, Uncle Jerry?" Rebecca exclaimed.

"Yes." He stifled a sob and continued. "I bought it for your Aunt Sarah fer Christmas. Now she don't need it, for there's no night there, where she is."

"You're right, Uncle Jerry." Rebecca gave him a squeeze.

"Well, it's night here," the intruding guest commented. "An' I mos' broke my back out in your stable rasslin' baled hay fer them hosses o' yourn with nuthin' but that smoky lantern fer light. Land, Jerry, if you don't git a hired man soon I'm goin' t' sell yer hosses, else you kin quit yer mopin' an' caterwaulin' an' feed 'em yerself, like yer usta. Who's yer young friend? One o' Sarah's nieces, I guess, by the sound o' things!"

"This here's Rebecca Randall, Aurelia's daughter, an' niece to Jane Sawyer," Jeremiah Cobb answered apologetically. "But she's bin like a daughter to Sarah an' me fer years—ain't ye, Becky?"

"You've been the daddy I never had, Uncle Jerry."

"Perkin' up, are ye?" observed the woman who disdained doing the stable chores. "Fust time I've heard you pleasant sence I come here yestiddy."

"And Becky, meet my big sister, Nettie Cobb. She's come from Acreville t' stay with me 'til I kin learn t' cook an' iron an sech."

"I didn't aim t' do the man's work round here, too," Miss Cobb sourly observed.

"I'd say you're pretty good at women's work, too, by the smell of those beans in the oven," offered Rebecca. "Yelloweyes, too, if my nose tells me right—my favorite. And, unless I miss my guess, Aunt Sarah made a crock o' dill pickles last fall, and they're under the cellar stairs waiting for me to find 'em. While you put the beans on and Uncle Jerry sets the table, I'll go get some." With that Rebecca grabbed the lantern and headed for the cellar door, leaving a speechless Nettie Cobb standing at the table.

When Rebecca returned from the cellar with a plate of pickles she found Uncle Jerry setting Aunt Sarah's blue willow plates and Patrick Henry silverware on the kitchen table's oilcloth, as Nettie, at the sideboard, sliced a steaming loaf of brown bread. Singing under her breath, Rebecca filled a tea ball with cut tea leaves from a can on the stove shelf and dropped it into Aunt Sarah's teapot. She filled it with hot water from the kettle and placed it on the table along with four earthenware mugs.

"Here. Take this to yer mother in tendin' the switchboard. She must be hungry."

Rebecca grinned and suppressed a giggle as she took the plate of beans and brown bread from the caustic Nettie. Miss Cobb's consideration shone through her calloused demeanor with an abruptness which startled Rebecca. She set the plate down long enough to add a couple of pickles and a cup of tea, then slipped off to the small front bedroom which had been converted into the telephone switchboard room.

"I see John got you here in one piece, Becky, honey," Aurelia greeted her as Rebecca entered and closed the hall door against the chill of the unheated passageway. "I was wonderin' if you'd forgotten me, but I guess Uncle Jerry needs all the comfortin' you can give him right now."

"Still using a cane, I see," Rebecca remarked, setting the plate and mug of tea on the table next to the switchboard, where Aurelia's cane was propped within reach.

"Actually, I walk pretty well without it now. I use it only when I have to go outdoors, like to walk over here."

"When're you coming home?" Rebecca inquired.

"I'm signin' off at eight, an' the phone company's movin' the switch panel out tomorrow durin' the funeral. Folks'll hafta limit their calls to their own party lines 'til it's hooked up at Watsons', some time nex' week."

"Where's the funeral?" Rebecca inquired. "I thought it would be here."

"Land sakes, no, Becky. Nettie won't have it. It'll be at the church at two o'clock. 'Sides, your Aunt Jane and I talked it over, an' we both felt it'd be best for Jeremiah to have the body out of the house. It's at Coombs Funeral Home in Wareham; they're bringin' Sarah back in her coffin on the train tomorrow mornin'. They don't need a hearse, since the burial will be in the cemetery behind the church, nex' to their daughter. My, but Nettie does know how t' fix beans! Are these some o' Sarah's pickles?"

"Sure are, Mother," Rebecca responded. "And the beans *do* smell good."

"Is Jerry eatin' enny?" Aurelia spoke quietly.

"Why, yes. He set the table while I went down for the pickles."

"I ain't an authority on psychology, but I think I know a bit about grief," Aurelia continued, "an' I told Jane that the sooner Nettie goes home the sooner Jerry'll perk up."

Rebecca was surprised to hear her mother speak so frankly, but she agreed. "She does seem rather direct," Rebecca answered. At that point the switchboard buzzed. "See you later, Mother." Rebecca kissed Aurelia's cheek and scooted for the kitchen.

"I'm ready t' eat," Nettie observed, as Rebecca was taking her seat. "Jerry says we don't eat in this house 'til we say grace, an' we don't say grace 'til everybody's at the table."

Rebecca bowed her head in silence, while Uncle Jerry offered a blessing.

"These'r good beans, Nettie," Jeremiah said after an awkward pause during which the only sound at the table was the clinking of china.

"You ain't et in two days. Anything tastes good when you're hungry," Nettie snapped.

"Miss Cobb," Rebecca said evenly but firmly, "You *do* make good beans, and the brown bread is good, too. I'm sure Uncle Jerry meant that as a compliment."

"What're we goin' t' put on you fer a suit fer the funeral tomorrow, Jerry?" his sister asked later as she was clearing the dishes while he stoked the stove. "Your suit coat has no trousers with it, an' them striped pants ain't fit to wear to a buryin'."

"Well, I ain't thought much about it," Jeremiah Cobb protested feebly.

"I just may have a solution," interrupted Rebecca, who had put her coat on to leave. "Just a minute—let me speak to Mother."

"Mother," Rebecca asked as soon as she had shut the door to the switchboard room behind her quietly, "Don't you have one of Father's old suits in your trunk?"

"I certainly do," Aurelia answered, guessing why Rebecca had asked. "And Lorenzo was about Jeremiah's build, too, though just a bit taller."

"Do . . . do you think he could wear it to Aunt Sarah's funeral tomorrow?"

"It'd be my pleasure," Aurelia responded warmly. "Jane an' I'll hafta fit it to him tonight, an' he can keep it for Sunday best, if he wants to. I've been thinkin' for years that somebody ought to get some use out o' that suit; it's silk an' wool—good stuff. He bought it in Boston."

"Uncle Jerry," Rebecca explained a moment later, "Mother's got a nice suit that no one in our family can wear, and she wants you to have it." Without waiting for him to protest, she went on, "Mother's got a long walk home at eight for a woman with a lame leg, and you'll need to come over to the brick house so's she and Aunt Jane can fit the suit to you. So if you'll see that she gets home, I'll go right now and dig the suit out." She shot a glance at the clock. "See you in an hour."

"Well, ain't she the blessedest creature you ever did see," Jeremiah remarked to his sister as Rebecca disappeared into the darkness of the woodshed. He shuffled to the kitchen door in time to see Rebecca emerge from the shed into the outdoors and hurry off up the street for the brick house.

A fresh breeze of mountain air had moved the fog created by the melting snow off toward the distant sea while they had been eating supper, and the moon shown in its brilliance across the winter landscape, so that he could watch Rebecca's flying tresses and flapping coat tails as she hurried up the street. Somewhere in the tired old man's heart a glimmer of hope had begun to glow.

17

THE RUIN OF ADAM LADD

Two days after Aunt Sarah's funeral found Rebecca riding in a car of the Portland & Montreal Railway rolling across the Maine winter landscape. It was a blustery day; winter was evidently set to return in all its fury. Rebecca watched the blowing snow chase itself across a frozen field, then she turned her thoughts back to the events of the past week.

Aunt Sarah had been laid to rest beneath Tory Hill, and Rebecca was unsure whether her heart ached more for her own loss of one so dear to her, or for Uncle Jerry's loss and the lonely life he must now face. Still, Mother and Aunt Jane would see that he got fed and properly clothed, Rebecca knew. His sister, Nettie, on the other hand, though tough enough when she wanted to appear so, had complained of feeling "aguish" the afternoon of the funeral, and she had caught the mail stage into Acreville the very next morning.

But Uncle Jerry would not have to feel beholden to the womenfolk of the brick house for the pies, mended pants, or ironed shirts they would bestow upon him. Rebecca had

had a long talk with him about this, and he understood that with the loss of Mark, and John away as a pre-medical student at Bowdoin, there were many uses for masculine assistance—wood to split, Dick-Boy and Molly and her calf to tend, drapes to hang during spring cleaning—so that he need never feel in their debt.

Jenny and Miss Maxwell had been overjoyed to see Rebecca, and she had been able to bunk for the night in Jenny's dorm room at Wareham Academy. Already in the weeks she had been a student there since Christmas, Jenny Randall had adjusted well to academic life, though she confessed to irritation at being constantly identified as "Rebecca's sister."

The train slowed to a crawl now, and Rebecca checked her watch: four o'clock. Dropping it on its chain into the pocket of her waistcoat, she inquired of the lady in the seat next to her what the matter might be.

"Construction," the woman said with evident irritation. "I ride this run several times a week, and we have been held up anywhere from twenty minutes to an hour at times. They're putting in a new wide-gauge track, and it will cross this line just up ahead."

"Do you mean the Boston & Down East?" Rebecca asked.

"That's the one," the woman answered knowingly. "Several of its directors have just been indicted for embezzling, so I guess the construction mess won't get cleared up for months—years maybe, the way these things drag on in the courts."

"Whatever are you talking about?" Rebecca inquired, trying to suppress her shock.

"Someone in your family own some railroad stock?" came the sarcastic query. The woman fished a copy of that morning's Portland *Press-Herald* from the pocket on the

The Portland & Montreal Railway rolled across the Maine winter landscape.

seat in front of her. It was folded to an article on the second page, and she passed it to Rebecca.

"New Road's Executives Indicted for Fraud," declared the headline. "Former Maine Man One of Three Named by FBI," cried the subheading.

The article told how a Boston grand jury had indicted the Boston & Down East's president, Jacob J. Heywood, for cheating stockholders by a scheme known as *overcapitalization.* Grand, inflated promises had been made about the value of the railway to small-town citizens in Maine and southern New Hampshire. Company shares had been sold on the American Stock Exchange at vastly inflated prices. Enough of this liquid cash had been spent on roadway construction to convince the public that the B. & D.E.R.R. was really a going enterprise. Too, thousands of dollars had been given to such charities as orphanages to maintain a false goodwill with the public, the article reported.

Even more money, perhaps as much as half the company's assets, had disappeared into the private bank accounts of several company executives, including that of Mr. Heywood and a vice president, Hamilton H. Aaronson. J. J. Heywood and H. H. Aaronson were even now in Boston's Suffolk County Jail. At their arraignment, the judge had declared that it "would be a mockery of justice to release them on bail," since the money used to make bail must necessarily come from stolen funds.

Rebecca burned with hurt and indignation when it occurred to her that the money used to purchase Sunnybrook Farm might have been stolen from folks like Aunt Jane Sawyer and Uncle Jerry Cobb, who had purchased stock certificates to save for their old age. She was fairly beside herself with shame and fear when she considered that Miss

Leonard's Home for Little Wayfarers had been partially underwritten by Boston & Down East's donations.

But she forced herself to read on. A young, "ambitious and clever" vice president, her own Adam Ladd, had reported Heywood and Aaronson to the authorities just after Christmas. Ladd had "cooperated fully with investigators," the article stated. But, "acting on a tip," a police detective had examined the depositors' records of the Massachusetts Bay City Bank. They had found nearly two hundred thousand deposited in the account of one Adam Ladd over two years' time—a sum far in excess of what he could have amassed from his known earnings and investments—and a warrant had been issued for his arrest. "Ladd's whereabouts are presently unknown," the article concluded.

With trembling hands, Rebecca crammed the newspaper back into its pocket. She, at least, would not be party to thievery, not even of the five-cent newspaper which had catalogued her fiance's sins.

Rebecca walked numbly across the marble tiles of Portland's downtown depot. Through tear-filled eyes, she sought the exit sign pointing her to the terminal of the uptown streetcar. A newsboy hawking the *Evening Express* blocked her path. "Read all about it, ma'am," he cried, "Crooked railway men go to jail!"

She fished out a nickel, took a paper, then scurried for the exit as the boy dived for the coin which she had let go before his hand got under it. Rebecca unfolded the newspaper as the streetcar clattered along Congress Street. She read only the sensational report that Adam had "fled Boston only moments ahead of police detectives," and he was thought to be "hiding out in rural Maine." She pushed the paper into the inside pocket of her coat and sought to quiet a throbbing headache by closing her eyes and leaning back.

Rebecca walked the cramps out of her traveling legs by hiking the two uphill city blocks from the streetcar stop to the Wayfarers' Home. Miss Edythe Leonard, lips set and white, met her at the door. "There's a gentleman here to see you," she said brusquely. "He's in my office."

Rebecca set herself for an interrogation by a police detective as she walked on rubber knees toward Miss Leonard's office halfway down the hall. Should she tell him how to find Aunt Mary's home in North Riverboro, where surely Adam must be hiding out, she pondered.

Rebecca opened the door gingerly and walked in. There stood Adam, dressed in a business suit, looking as dapper as ever, though evidently more than a little worried. He met her in the center of the room and grasped her arms. "Rebecca, have you seen the paper?" he cried.

"If you mean *this,* yes." She drew out the *Express,* and he snatched it from her shaking fingers.

He looked at her helplessly. "What can I say? I had no idea I was wanted by the police until I read the *Press-Herald* on the train this afternoon, coming in from Boston. Now the *Express* even has me *escaping* capture by fleeing to Maine. Surely a criminal who is known in Maine as well as I would think of a more original place to spend his ill-gotten gains while on the run than here, don't you think?"

"I don't know what to think." It was Rebecca's turn to be helpless.

"Before I say more, let me inform you that Miss Leonard has also read the *Press-Herald.* She has not called the police only because she knew that you were expected this afternoon, and she wanted you to have a chance to 'confront' me, as she put it. She is even now sitting by the phone in the parlor; the minute I step outside this office, she has promised she will phone the authorities—and I believe her! Incidentally," he added lowering his voice, "how many phones are there in this house?"

"Two—this one, and the one in the parlor," Rebecca answered.

"Same line?"

"Yes, why?"

"I have an idea."

"You *are* in a fix, Adam." Rebecca's heart was filled with sympathy for Adam. Yet, in her head, all she had been taught, all she had ever learned about honesty, integrity, paying one's debt to society said he was getting exactly what he deserved. "But why, Adam, *why* did you do it?"

"If I told you that the newspapers are wrong, that the detectives are wrong, that the grand jury was lied to, that I have committed no crime, then would you believe me?"

"Have I ever refused to believe anything you told me?"

"And there's the rub," said Adam. "You believe me in your heart, but your head says I must be guilty of *something,* or else I would not have been indicted. And that leads to why I came to Portland today. When I left Boston I had not been indicted, so far as I knew, but I did know that an investigator was looking into some supposed evidence and that I might be arrested soon. But on the way here I thought better of my plan; yet I still felt I must see you, that I should tell you face-to-face that I am innocent of all wrongdoing, and that when this is over the Boston & Down East Railroad will survive, prosper, and even repay those who have been robbed by its directors."

"What do you mean, Adam, 'plan'?"

"That would be telling too much at this point. I can only say that you, Miss Leonard, and Aunt Mary can all expect to be subpoenaed as witnesses. You may choose to ignore the subpoena, since it is across a state line and it is unlikely that you will be arrested, but to do so would certainly put me in jail."

"What . . . what do you want of me—and the others?"

"Just come to the trial and tell the truth. There will be dates and places to recall, and you and the others must corroborate each other's stories. But I cannot jeopardize my chances or compromise the truth by telling you in advance what I think you will be asked. You can be assured that the prosecutor will question you closely, and he will want to know if you and I have collaborated on our answers."

"I have nothing to hide."

"Exactly. And your straightforward answers will win out over any falsehood in the finish." Adam checked his watch, then he stepped to the window. "Right on time."

"What is on time?"

"My cab. When I saw you coming up the walk, I used Miss Leonard's phone to call a cab, and I asked him to be here in twenty minutes."

"But where will you go? North Riverboro?"

"Boston, to surrender to the police. I don't care to languish for a month in the Portland City Jail waiting extradition papers from Boston. The wheels of justice, as I'm sure you've heard, turn rather slowly. I hope to speed them up a bit by turning myself in to the proper authorities."

"But you said Miss Leonard . . ."

"Don't worry about Miss Leonard." Adam squeezed Rebecca's hand, then he kissed it, patted it, squeezed it again. "You'll hear from me soon. I'll write—perhaps a telegram." Having said that, Adam removed the receiver from the cradle of Miss Leonard's desk phone, laying it on the desk. "Leave the office ahead of me—go down the hall and tell Miss Leonard that I'm leaving now—now go!"

Adam drew a high, straight-backed chair against the office door, just under the knob, tipping it with its weight against the inside as he pulled the door shut after himself. He paused only long enough to check the door; it was braced as securely from within as if he had locked it.

"Miss Leonard, Mr. Ladd is leaving," Rebecca called as she entered the parlor. She need not have spoken, for Edythe Leonard, who had been watching her office door, was already cranking the wall phone, trying in desperation to reach an operator. "That . . . that scoundrel!" she cried. "He's taken the phone off the cradle in my office. I can't call out!" She slammed the receiver onto its hook and dived for the hall holding her skirts in both hands as the heels of her high-buttoned shoes kicked out. Rebecca let her pass, then hurried after her.

"Rebecca! Miss Randall! The door's braced from the inside."

Rebecca heard Miss Leonard's cries, but her heart was set on an urgent mission of her own. She reached the front door and opened it in time to see the door of the hansom slam shut. The cab made a U-turn in the street; "Hup," cried the driver, and with a quick trot the rig jounced off into the night.

Rebecca drew her coat closer against the raw air of the sea, the east wind folding back under the westward-moving storm, bringing with it snow and stinging sleet that would soon hide the grimy cobblestones and soot-blackened buildings of the city. She waited until the clatter of hooves faded in the distance, and only the hum and whistle of the wind in the telephone wires and bare elms broke the quiet.

Presently Rebecca walked inside where she found Miss Leonard fairly dancing with fury as Rose Dowe, another matron, used a table knife to unscrew the office doorknob.

"You let him get away," Miss Leonard snapped, shaking her finger at Rebecca. "You'll answer to the police for this!"

"Miss Leonard, please – he said he was leaving, and I told you at once. What more could I have done?"

"Miss Randall's right, Miss Leonard," said Rose, pulling the knob off and giving the door a shove. "I heard her tell you myself. Miss Randall was halfway to the parlor before this fellow even left your office."

"Nevertheless, she's going to talk to the police!"

"I'll tell the police all I know," Rebecca replied. She realized then that she was shaking, and she struggled to maintain her composure as she spoke. "Mr. Ladd, as a matter of fact, said that you and I can expect to be subpoenaed as witnesses at his trial."

"What could we possibly know that would help him?"

"Could it have anything to do with the fact that Wayfarers' Home has taken grant money from the railroad?" meekly suggested Rose Dowe.

"Why . . . why . . . if that gets in the papers. . . ." Her voice broke off. She sat down at her desk and replaced the receiver onto its hook. She drummed her fingers angrily on the mahogany desk. "Why, no. On the other hand, if Ladd thinks that giving to charity will save his neck. . . ." She picked up the phone by its stem. Bending over, Miss Leonard turned the crank on the oak box on the end of her desk. "I'm calling the police, anyway," she said decisively.

There was nothing that Rebecca could tell Portland City Police Detective Johnson about Adam Ladd pertinent to the case, other than what he'd read in the papers. "He said he was going back to Boston to turn himself in," Rebecca said, fighting back tears. "His only purpose in coming here was to tell me to my face that he loves me and that he's fighting the charges, since he's innocent."

"They're all innocent," Johnson growled. He checked his watch, "The 'Flying Yankee' pulled out of the depot on the southbound track twenty minutes ago." Without asking permission, he picked up Miss Leonard's phone. "Central—Johnson here—Portland P.D. Put me through to the depot master."

Sergeant Johnson put the phone down with a thud. "Ladd made the Boston train, all right," he grumbled. "I'll stop at Western Union on the way back to the station and wire the Boston P.D. that he's coming. And by the way, Miss Randall, you can be sure that if you have any bank accounts in your name, the police will be scrutinizing your deposits and withdrawals."

As for Adam Ladd, he had anticipated Johnson's telegram to the Boston police. Adam got off the train in Somerville and took a streetcar into Boston, where he spent the night in his own bed. He went to the police the next day in the company of his attorney, after learning that the judge had finally released Heywood and Aaronson on bail, pending the trial. Like the others, Adam Ladd was given his freedom upon posting bond.

18

BELLS RING ON TORY HILL

Rebecca had never seen a forsythia bush in bloom, nor had she heard the evening call of a mourning dove as a child at Sunnybrook or while she was growing up at the brick house in Riverboro. Neither at Wareham, where the pigeons cooed along the sidewalks of the academy, did she hear the plaintive call of these springtime birds, for they belonged to a climate milder than that of inland Maine.

She was amazed in early April, therefore, to awaken at dawn one glorious morning to a new song, sung by turtle-doves as pleasant as those who sang in Solomon's Song of Songs—a haunting cooing unlike anything she'd ever heard before. Rebecca slid from her bed and opened her window. There it was again: "Cooo, coo-oo; cooo, coo-oo; cooo, coo-oo!" The air was mild; as a matter of fact the thermometer she had installed outside her window said it was nearly fifty. At a quarter past five, it would be more than an hour before her girls would stir. So, quickly she dressed and slipped downstairs.

The morning was still, and the weathervane on top of the spire of a distant church pointed inland, to the southwest. A light perfume of spring blossoms was in the air, not the sharp sea smell of too-old fish which drifted from the harbor on the easterly breeze, but the odor of flowers of unknown species. Just around the block Rebecca found a hedge of shrubs, dressed in brilliant yellow, and in the yard a tree in bloom with brilliant lavender tulip-shaped blossoms.

Rebecca had learned already that Maine seaside winters are not the winters of the frigid interior. Warmed by the Gulf Stream's current, the shoreline of the North Atlantic experiences milder weather than beyond the coastal hills, a mere five miles from the sea. When Riverboro or Temperance or Wareham got a blizzard, the same storm might produce rain and driving wind in Portland or Brunswick or Rockland. Already by mid-March the yards of Munjoy Hill were bare of snow, and gardens even had toads hopping about on sunny days, though a letter from her mother near the end of March had told how the upper Saco Valley was still under its heavy winter blanket and the river still locked in ice. "I must warn Fanny daily," Mother had written, "not to cross the brook on the ice on her way home from school lest she step on a rotten spot and fall through."

Yet, only last week, several of Rebecca's orphan charges had merrily gone wading in a city creek on their way home from school, hiking their skirts above their knees and soiling their bloomers in the filthy drainage water. Though Rebecca had scolded them, she had laughed within herself, remembering her own childish folly at Sunnybrook—drenching herself to her armpits as she and older sister Hannah tended their froggery in a pool along the creek's bank.

Springlike weather comes nearly a month earlier here, thought Rebecca, as she took note of the tulips and crocuses, the pussy willows along the drainage ditch, and the swelling buds of an old sugar maple which shaded a neighbor's yard in summer. *And what a glorious morning! Will my life ever again be as glorious as this spring day?* she mused.

Rebecca had not seen Adam Ladd since he left in haste in January, though they had expected to plan their wedding over St. Valentine's Day. The terms of his bailment would not then permit him to leave Massachusetts; and though he had hinted that he might send her a round-trip ticket to Boston ("There's an intimate little cafe just off the Common; we can worship together at Park Street Church on Sunday," he had written), he had retracted even this half-offer in his next letter, stating that "the lawyers are eating up all my available cash, and the court has tied up my savings."

Construction was continuing on the new Sunnybrook Station of the Boston & Down East Railroad, Rebecca had heard from her mother, who corresponded with an old neighbor near Sunnybrook Farm. Adam confirmed that the tracks were being laid and trestles were being built. "And it looks as though the work won't be held up more than a couple of months." He explained that the judge had delayed bankruptcy proceedings, if necessary at all, until after the trial. The judge had also ruled that completion of the nearly finished road would serve the best interests of stockholders. Since the railroad was a government franchise, funds had been put in escrow toward the laying of as many miles of track as necessary.

Neither Rebecca nor Miss Leonard had received a subpoena to testify at Adam's trial, a fact which both puzzled and troubled Rebecca. He had been very insistent that their testimony would be crucial to prove his innocence. The months had dragged by, and Adam had written of delays and postponements and motions for discovery of evidence.

Rebecca's mail that April morning brought a square envelope of linen parchment postmarked Riverboro and dated the previous day. "What can this be?" she wondered aloud. "I know of no weddings planned in Riverboro for this spring."

She slit the thick envelope open to find that it contained still another envelope, in which was a silver-embossed card covered with tissue paper. "Pretty fancy stuff," Rebecca told herself. "Only the Watsons and the Meserves would spend money on such vanity. Persis Watson is being courted by my brother John, but she's only seventeen and he's in college—not them, surely! And I doubt that Huldah Meserve'd even send me an invitation."

The card read:

Mrs. Aurelia Randall

and

Mr. Jeremiah Cobb

Request the Honour of Your Presence

At the Celebration of Their Marriage

Tory Hill Meeting House

Riverboro, Maine

Saturday, the Twenty-Third of May

In the Year of Our Lord 1895

At Two o'clock in the Afternoon

Reception to Follow at the Brick House

Aurelia had enclosed a letter, tucked just inside:

Dearest Rebecca,

Lest you feel Uncle Jerry and I are acting in haste, please be assured that we are both adults. Be assured also that we have had some long and serious talks with Mr. Baxter, and he agrees that it's the right thing for us to do.

Your father once told me that, were he to die, the greatest honor I could do him would be to marry again and show folks that I was happy enough in my first marriage to want to marry again. We were happy, Lorenzo and I, though we had our trials, some of which are well known.

Two questions I have asked myself in order to find the answer to a third and more important one: First, can I make Jerry happy? Second, do I love him? If the answer to both these questions is yes (and it is!), then I believe in our case the answer to the third question—is this God's will?—will likewise be yes.

I do not believe marriages are *made* in heaven, Rebecca. Rather, they are *conceived* in heaven in the mind of God. But they are, very realistically, *made* here on earth, as a couple yields to God's plan for their lives. Otherwise, they reject that plan and strike out in their own selfish way, often to their *unmaking.*

Please do not think me a sentimental old widow for wanting a church wedding, Rebecca. And yes, I will wear a white dress. I recently found your grandmother's silk wedding dress in a trunk where she had stored it many years ago, and it is still in beautiful condition, even after washing and ironing. Fortunately, my mother was a large woman, even as a girl, for Jane found it necessary to resew some seams, but there was material enough all the same to go around my no-longer-girlish figure, and it now fits me marvelously. You may wish to have Aunt Jane remake it for your wedding, if the old silk doesn't shred and tear from my using it! I'm surprised that it still holds together after all these years, as silk is a very fragile material.

As I'm sure you know, your father and I didn't have what could be called a proper wedding. We eloped, just the way you read about in books, with a ladder (your grandfather's haymow ladder!) to my bedroom window, and then we walked nearly all night until daylight to get to Maplewood, since Lorenzo didn't own a horse. We were married in Maplewood by a justice of the peace.

I wouldn't recommend marrying like your father and I did to anybody. I'm sure we had more good days than bad ones during those early years, but the bad ones were miserable times indeed! If the Lord hadn't shut up my womb for the four years until Hannah was born, I'm afraid I might have ended as wretchedly as Abijah Flagg's mother.

Had my first child been a boy, I had every intention of naming him Samuel, like in the Bible. But since I got a girl, I named her Hannah, after Samuel's mother, whose womb the Lord opened.

But beyond the sentimental, I believe a church wedding to be a witness to the community that a bride is a picture of Christ's Bride, His church. This is not to criticize Emma Jane for marrying in our barn, for the building is not the church in the true sense, but the body of believers who meet to worship is the church. It's just that I feel more comfortable marrying in a church building.

Christ's Bride (His people, not any individual) is a chaste bride, and I came to Lorenzo a chaste bride, and I am going to Jerry a chaste bride, and that's the real reason I wish to wear white.

I have asked your brother John to walk me down the aisle and give me away in the name of all my children. I got his letter from Brunswick just this A.M., and he says he'll be glad to do so.

Jane is my attendant. Jeremiah has asked Bill Perkins to be his best man, and I think he'll agree, though he says he thinks Jerry's a "thundering old fool" for going along with my church wedding idea.

I hate to bring this up, but is the wedding still on with you and Adam Ladd? It hurts me very much to hear what folks are saying about him around the village. I guess I've asked a silly question, haven't I? Because of course you can't make any plans until you see what will happen in Boston.

Your Loving Mother

❧ ❧ ❧

No more beautiful a bride ever walked the aisle of Tory Hill Meeting House than Aurelia. That was the consensus of a group of elderly ladies. "I once told Mrs. Deacon Sawyer if ever her daughters gets hitched, the hull town'll be so jealous of their beauty that half the womenfolk'll go home mad," cackled the ancient Widow Trask as she leaned on her cane. "You're next, Jane dearie," the old woman chuckled as she came through the receiving line. "If Miranda hadn't a-bin in sech a tear to hurry off t' her reward, she'd 'a' found a man, too, I'm sure. And who's this young man that give ye away?" she said, with a wink at John.

"John, my eldest son," Aurelia explained, unsure whether Mrs. Trask was teasing or actually senile.

"Ayuh! I knew it. He's the very image of Is'el Sawyer. Tain't everybuddy that gets t' start their home with their kids all growed. I think it's better that way—get 'em full grown, then raise 'em down 'stead o' up. Then by the time they're babies, you kin raise them back up, and you'll know fer shouh how they'll turn out." She moved on, giggling like a schoolgirl at her own silly joke.

The receiving line finished their handshaking and hugging and kissing and "congratulations" and "God bless your new home." The crowd had begun to dwindle, as two by two, or in threes and fours, families in buggies and surries and buckboards or on foot or horseback or bicycle moved off toward the brick house in the village for punch and wedding cake.

Rebecca had sent Fanny and Jenny on ahead to cut and pour and serve, and sister Hannah and husband Will had likewise left with Dick-Boy and the surrey to look after the gifts and the guest book. She had worked until past midnight each of the three nights since she had arrived from Portland, helping wherever she was most needed—hemming Aunt Jane's maid-of-honor dress, making silk flowers for decorations, meeting Hannah and Will at the Maplewood depot, tending Hannah's baby so Hannah could help the village ladies with Uncle Jerry's spring cleaning—a process which was capped by wallpapering the Cobb sitting room and bedroom.

Rebecca found herself without a responsibility at the reception, except to collapse into a meetinghouse pew and watch the photographer hired from Wareham take wedding photos. As unofficial general overseer of last-minute preparations, she had nearly reached what Aunt Jane sometimes described as a "nervous breakdown."

But for reasons she wouldn't even let herself think about, the ordinarily gregarious Rebecca now wanted to be alone. Perhaps it was her months of mothering three dozen girls, and the realization that when she returned on Monday the halls and the dorm and the playground would be as empty as her heart, for even now the orphans were leaving for the farms. Possibly it was the consideration that, for her, the possibilities of having the pleasure of marriage seemed to be moving further and further beyond her horizon.

Whatever her reasons, Rebecca waited in the church until the last carriage had moved out of the yard, except for the wedding party. She then set out on a leisurely stroll toward the brick house, hoping to arrive there after a goodly number of the guests had departed.

Rebecca walked down the road toward the village, and soon she rounded a bend in the road, leaving the meetinghouse behind. The road ahead dipped, and the brick house would not come in sight until she mounted the grade beyond. The trotting of a horse and the rattle of carriage wheels caught her attention. Without looking up, she stepped onto the shoulder to let the vehicle pass.

But the rig did not pass. "Ride to the brick house, miss?" called the driver. It was Adam!

Rebecca was torn between a desire to leap into the seat beside him and embrace and kiss him, and a restraint almost touching on revulsion which caused her to hold back. She paused for a frozen moment; then fearing an awkward situation which might embarrass them both, she clambered aboard.

"Beautiful wedding," he said with no apparent emotion.

"Were you there?" Rebecca was shocked.

"Your mother invited me." He produced an invitation like the one she had herself received, and Rebecca recognized her mother's handwriting in Adam's Boston address.

"I sat in the balcony and slipped out early. I'm not going to humiliate you or your family by going to the reception."

"But I . . . I thought . . ."

"You thought I was free only on bail and subject to arrest if I left Massachusetts. And so I am, except that I am in Maine with the judge's permission, because of the peculiar circumstance of my being needed in this state to enable the Boston & Down East Railroad to make certain business transactions."

"Meaning?"

"It's a bit complicated. But as I'm sure you know, the railroad now operates under a court-appointed trustee. This arrangement, however, while fully workable in Massachusetts—where the railroad's business address is—will not meet all the legal requirements for Maine. And since I have not been indicted in Maine, the Maine courts have not seen fit to take over certain of the railroad's property options registered with me as trustee."

"All of which means?"

"As I said, it's complicated. I am in Maine on business; I signed some papers yesterday in the courthouse in Portland under the supervision of the judge's secretary. I have until noon Monday to check in with the judge in Boston. Actually, the secretary tried to get me on the train Friday evening, but since he has no legal power to hold me while in Maine, I told him as politely as I could to go to Boston by himself. If I'm not there Monday, I'm sure the judge will issue a bench warrant for my arrest." Adam slapped the reins. "Get up!" he said to the horse. "I've got to get this rented rig back to Wareham by dark," he told Rebecca.

"Have . . . have you stopped to see your Aunt Mary?"

"I spent last night with her. She believes me guilty, because she cannot understand how anyone can become as wealthy as I seem to have become without somehow being dishonest. But Aunt Mary has a big heart. She's promised to pray for me daily."

"I'm praying for you, Adam. But how . . . how is your trial coming?"

Adam smiled wryly. "We've got a date at last—next week, Wednesday, at nine in the morning."

"Am I going to be asked to testify?"

"Not at this juncture. Most likely you won't be needed. I've been able to turn up other witnesses with the help of a private detective." Adam drew the rig up at the brick house's drive without turning in. He squeezed Rebecca's hand and looked directly into her eyes. "Rebecca, I love you."

Rebecca looked at the seat between them, then she gazed across the river, at the clouds scudding in the spring sky. If she were up there with the clouds, she could see the ocean—silly thought! But if she were up where God is, she could see the future—and Adam's heart. But dare she trust her own?

Rebecca returned his gaze. "I love you, Adam. I always will." With that she leaped from the chaise and ran in the shed door, slipped through the kitchen, and up to her room.

The moon was up and the stars were out when Aunt Jane rapped on Rebecca's door. "The guests are gone, Rebecca. There's a fire in the kitchen stove an' hot water in the reservoir. Come down an' wash up an' we'll have a plate of yelloweyes."

19

THE TRIAL OF ADAM LADD

Rebecca returned to Portland on Monday to find the Wayfarers' Home nearly empty. She had left the previous week only after readying those orphans in her charge for their summer of farm work. There had been duffel bags to pack, clothes to mend, tearful youngsters to kiss and hug and pat and admonish to work hard and mind their manners.

The very morning Rebecca had taken the early train out of the Portland depot for Maplewood, she had seen several upcountry farmers' wives disembark from points north, and she suspected they were heading for Wayfarers' Home to choose a Johnny or a Susie, a Heidi or a Hans to work in the gardens, to follow the cows to summer pasture, or to pitch hay and pick corn until school opened in Portland again nearly five months later. Rebecca, her heart aching for her orphans, her children whom she had loved and tucked into bed and prayed with and sung to all winter, had avoided these farm wives, letting them fend for themselves to find Munjoy Hill the same way she had more than a year earlier. She was on her way to her mother's wedding. She had left with the fretful blessing of Edythe Leonard, who, exasperated at Rebecca's request for time off during such a busy season, had been placated only when Rebecca had herself found two local volunteers to take her place.

Now it was the Tuesday after the wedding, and Rebecca rose at daybreak. She passed the empty beds in her dorm, crossed the upstairs hall, and dragging a chair in one hand and carrying her Bible in the other, she slipped onto the narrow balcony with its wrought-iron railing. Gathering her corduroy robe about her shoulders, she began to read from Christ's Sermon on the Mount. After some moments, she came to the verse ordinarily identified as the Golden Rule: "All things whatsoever ye would that men should do to you, do ye even so to them: for this is the law and the prophets." Rebecca closed her Bible and prayed briefly, though her heart was not in her prayer; truly, she doubted that God had heard her.

Returning to her room, Rebecca dressed. Seeing that it was an hour yet to breakfast, she decided to slip down to the kitchen for an early cup of coffee.

Here she found Sophie, an orphaned girl of about her own age who was now on the Wayfarers' Home staff, lighting the gas range to bake breakfast biscuits. "I'm happy as a boid," Sophie chortled, her Brooklyn dialect so accented with her native Hungarian tongue that Rebecca had to strain to make out her words, "Ve get da day off."

"Why are you so happy?" Rebecca inquired, ladling several measures of ground coffee into a blue agate pitcher.

"Ve get da day off!" Sophie repeated.

"The day off? Oh! Oh, really? Why?"

"'Cause da kids iss gone. Miss Leonard says ve kin hev t'day t' rest, soon's breakfast iss done. Cleanup starts tomorra."

Rebecca was disappointed and indignant. After nearly a week's absence, she had begun this day determined to bury herself in work to forget her troubles. Now she was expected to take a holiday.

As she waited for the coffee to steep, Rebecca noticed a Bible-verse motto hanging in its frame above a worktable. It was Matthew 7:12, Christ's words in the Golden Rule, which she had read earlier on the balcony. Yet something, it occurred to Rebecca, was missing, for the verse was not complete, and she knew at once what it was: *for this is the law and the prophets.* That was the clincher—the entire weight of the Old Testament rested on doing right by one's neighbor, Christ had said. Remove one commandment, and like stones in an arch, the others fall with it. Two-thirds of the Bible would be rejected out-of-hand if Rebecca selfishly sought her own ends instead of the good of others.

And while Rebecca was thinking on the weighty truth she had just discovered, her mind ran ahead—who should she most honor, next to God? Her thoughts stopped at the one she had pledged to put first in her life in a lifetime love relationship—Adam Ladd.

Here I am feeling sorry for myself, and I've been given a holiday to do what I ought most to do—to be at Adam's side in his trial tomorrow, Rebecca told herself, almost out loud. She flew up the steps two at a time as she ran to Miss Leonard's bedroom to boldly explain her decision. What was two extra days off at a time like this?

At seven-thirty Rebecca was boarding the "Flying Yankee" bound for Boston when she remembered the coffee in the agate pitcher. "Sophie will wonder why I left without waiting for it to boil," she mused. "I am off to more important things than morning coffee."

❧ ❧ ❧

"You shouldn't have come," Adam told her as he greeted her outside the courtroom door on Wednesday morning.

"It's only right that I should be here," Rebecca responded warmly, squeezing his hand.

His only response was to fight back tears, then pull her aside to let three arrogant-looking men crowd ahead of them into the courtroom. "That's A. G. Arnold, and those other men, I presume, are his lawyers," Adam said huskily, indicating a tall, poker-faced gentleman slightly older than he. "He's another vice president, the one who hasn't been indicted, and he's not speaking to me; when you hear him on the witness stand you'll soon know why. I've had a private detective on the case for the past month, and my attorney has had Arnold subpoenaed as a witness—a rather reluctant one, I must say."

The Suffolk County prosecutor made out a pretty convincing *prima facie* case against Adam. He produced a bank statement of an account in Adam Ladd's name, listing deposits over the past year and a half totaling some two hundred thousand. And the dates and amounts of the deposits corresponded with deficits discovered in an audit of the account of the Boston & Down East Railroad. Further incriminating evidence included a bank book of the same account, found during a police search of a filing cabinet in Adam's office.

Adam, on the witness stand, produced a letter he had written to Aunt Mary from Portland on the very day he was alleged to have been present in Boston to make a substantial deposit at the Massachusetts Bay City Bank. On cross examination, the prosecutor tried to trick Adam into admitting that "a friend" in Portland had actually posted the letter for him in order to establish an alibi, but Adam would not crack under pressure. Though he had been near tears before the trial, Rebecca could see that he now had control of himself.

The disputed but substantial alibi seemed to impress the judge, the Honorable Ezra Winthrop. Judge Winthrop was impressed, too, when the teller who had initialed several deposit transactions admitted that to his "best recollection" he had never seen Adam Ladd until that day in court. The entire case against Adam unraveled when a second bank teller pointed out A. G. Arnold as the "Mr. Ladd" who had made several deposits at Massachusetts Bay City Bank. The signatures on the deposit receipts, though similar to Adam's, were shown by a handwriting expert to be forgeries.

Arnold, when on the witness stand, at first claimed to have been at the bank on "other important business" on the dates in question. His alibi collapsed entirely, however, when a bank vice president testified that Arnold had no account there in his own name.

Judge Winthrop dismissed all charges at once, and he made Adam a co-manager of the railway's assets, shared jointly with a court-appointed trustee until Arnold, J. J. Heywood, and H. H. Aaronson could be brought to trial.

❧ ❧ ❧

"But how did Mr. Arnold think he could get away with using your name?" exclaimed an exasperated, puzzled Rebecca later. She and Adam were ensconced in the "intimate cafe" beside Boston Common he had mentioned in his letter, waiting for their orders of spring lamb chops and baked potatoes.

"Aliases are easy enough to come by," Adam patiently explained. "Much of Boston's criminal activity is by men with assumed names."

"But *your* name! How could he use *your* bank book?"

"It was my name, but it certainly wasn't my bank book!" Adam cautioned her. "I was unaware of its existence until I was arrested after he planted it in my filing cabinet. As for his being able to make withdrawals, so long as the forged signature on withdrawal slips matched the forged signature on the bank's records, he could have spent the money, and I'd have been none the wiser—unless of course I tried to open an account at Massachusetts Bank."

"But what if he'd used a fictitious name?" asked Rebecca.

"Then it's unlikely the police would have found the bank account, and he might have been able to spend the money, with interest, when he got out of jail. But I choose to believe that 'what if's' exist only in our finite minds. There are no 'what if's' in the plans of God. We reap what we sow. Perfect crimes exist only in the imaginations of fiction writers."

"And in the minds of criminals who haven't yet been caught," chuckled Rebecca.

"I guess that proves another truth," Adam remarked.

"What is that?" asked Rebecca.

"That the wicked flee when no man pursues them," said Adam. "Arnold used my name out of no spite to me, I'm sure. He thought he'd be able to put the police off-track by framing me, even tipping the bank examiner to the bogus account although he wasn't himself being prosecuted—and it backfired!"

❧ ❧ ❧

Rebecca and Adam strolled hand in hand across the Common under maples with new leaves now opened full. For a while they watched the swans and ducks glide across the pond, then for a quarter each, they rode in a paddle-boat on the small lake. They crossed the Common again to the corner of Tremont and Park. Here an Italian organ grinder cranked his hurdy-gurdy as his monkey scampered about with a tin cup. Adam tossed the creature a dime, and its master cranked out an Old-World tune.

"You told me you give gospel concerts here on the Common with your violin?" Rebecca inquired.

"I do indeed. On this very corner, once or twice a week all summer, as a ministry." He pointed to the imposing red-brick edifice at the intersection, its five-tiered white spire pointing heavenward just across Park Street from where they stood. "That's my church—The Park Street Church. Numbers of our members minister here to the crowds that pass by, on foot or by trolley," Adam said, indicating the ceaseless stream of crowded streetcars wheeling past, their electric terminals screeching and showering sparks onto the street, their side curtains rolled up for ventilation during the hot spring afternoon.

"I passed here on my way to my room at the Shawmut Hotel yesterday," Rebecca said in surprise. "I had no idea this was your church."

"You've come at a good time to visit 'Brimstone Corner,'" he chuckled. "Our pastor, Rev. Isaac Lansing, is speaking on Christian marriage at tonight's evening service. I'd find it a lot more meaningful if you were with me."

"Of course!" Rebecca found herself enthusiastic about being with Adam for the first time in several months. "But why is it called 'Brimstone Corner?' The preaching?"

"Actually, Pastor Lansing does preach all facets of the gospel," Adam answered with a laugh. "But gunpowder was stored in an armory here during the Revolutionary War. After the armory was torn down in 1809 to make room for this church, the name stuck. For the Park Street Church resulted from revivals in three Boston churches in those days, and it was evident that the fire of the Lord was upon the new congregation."

The couple crossed Park Street and passed the church. Through an iron gate they entered the Old Granary Burial Ground. Here Rebecca was enthralled by a sense of oneness with her own heritage as they paused briefly at the graves of Paul Revere, Samuel Adams, and the parents of Benjamin Franklin. Then, as they sat together on a marble bench, Rebecca pointed to the simple inscription on a black slate grave marked: "Mary Goose."

"Some say that she was the real Mother Goose who lent her name to the nursery rhymes," chuckled Adam. "But nobody knows for sure, I suppose."

"Can I . . . can we ever know for sure the things we once thought we knew?" inquired Rebecca.

"What do you mean?"

"Once a man asked me to marry him, and I said yes," Rebecca answered earnestly. "Mother Goose had her nest—-shall I ever have mine?"

Long sat the lovers in the historic cemetery until the lengthening shadows brought the chill of a New England spring evening across the old Boston Common. "Can we . . . can we pick up the pieces and make some wedding plans, now that this nightmare is behind us?" Adam asked hesitantly.

"You know we can, darling!"

20

A SUNNYBROOK HONEYMOON

"Adam, those children deserve a better life than being confined to a city orphanage," Rebecca remarked one June day as she and Adam sat in a Portland seaside cafe looking out on the islands of Casco Bay. Now that most of the orphans were gone for the summer, Rebecca's responsibilities were lightened. Besides presenting the organization's work to churches and civic groups one or two evenings a week, she had most evenings free to spend with Adam, as well as all day Saturdays.

Adam had taken a semi-permanent room in Portland's Eastland Hotel, because, with the finishing work to be done on the roadbed of the Boston & Down East, it was imperative that he spend most of his time in Maine. Sunnybrook Station outside Temperance would be completed within a month, and the first train would run across the fields of the old Randall farm right after Labor Day.

The railroad did not need to sue for bankruptcy after all, much to Adam's relief. Heywood, Aaronson, and Arnold were now in jail, and most of the funds which they had pilfered had been recovered from the various bank accounts where they had concealed it under assumed names; only Arnold had had the audacity to use another's name to hide his illegal account. And, with the return of the monies, the company now had more money than it needed to build its road, since it had been over-funded to begin with. So, with the court's permission, Adam bought the entire Saco & Androscoggin River Railroad's narrow-gauge line, not only the tracks from Temperance to Maplewood, but the main line into Brunswick. Now, after buying a right-of-way to build tracks from Maplewood to Riverboro, Adam set his engineers at work planning a new, standard-gauge rail system which would stretch from the foothills of the White Mountains to the Atlantic coast, providing rapid transportation by which farms could easily market their produce. Within two years, Adam's surveyors told him, the old, two-hour stagecoach run from Maplewood to Riverboro could be replaced by a train covering that distance in twenty minutes.

And Adam Ladd, the Boston & Down East's only executive not corrupted by the cash excess, was now made the company's president and chief executive officer by a vote of the stockholders.

But, "I'd like to help run an orphanage, not merely to serve on a children's home's board of directors," Adam told Rebecca that evening in the cafe. "The railroad is well on its way to success, and there are many men who can replace me as head of this outfit. And I'm sure I have friends in both Boston and Portland who would gladly help fund a new orphanage. What do you say we find us a country place and set up a farm home where homeless kids won't have to readjust to being shipped off to farms every spring, then back to the city in the fall?" Adam spoke flippantly, almost in glee. But deep down, Rebecca felt, he was sounding out her own feelings on the matter.

"Adam," she said, "the brick house is empty once again, except for Aunt Jane, now that Mother is married and John and Jenny are away. It would make a perfect home for homeless children!"

The stars came out over Casco Bay as Rebecca and Adam sipped sodas and nibbled at their strawberry shortcake. Here and there the twinkle of a distant, lighted window showed where an island beach cottage was already opened up for the summer season. A bright-lit ferry boat came down the channel, its steam engine throbbing as it slid steadily between the islands and through the calm harbor waters toward its berth at the city dock just below where the lovers were seated.

Rebecca touched Adam's arm and pointed. "Look!" she whispered. "The vessel that left its 'little harbor' for the stormy sea is back, safe at last in its home port."

"A ship is a restless vessel; it will soon set sail again," mildly protested Adam.

"But it will not sail alone this time." Rebecca wiped her mouth on her napkin, then she blew out the lamp at their table so that they could more easily watch the harbor lights.

❧ ❧ ❧

Now that Adam's trial was settled and the courts had released their liens on his bank account, Rebecca and Adam had reconsidered a June wedding; but June had come and gone. Fourth of July, Independence Day, Adam took the day off, but not to celebrate. Instead, he caught the streetcar to Munjoy Hill, where Rebecca met him at the stop, and they walked together to Wayfarers' Home. "We'll watch the fireworks at the waterfront this evening," he told her as she ushered him into the parlor.

"Meanwhile, we have a few things to discuss," Rebecca said lightly. "I hope your tracks are smooth and straight, 'cause I intend to travel on a full head of steam. The second Sunday in August is 'Old Home Day' at Tory Hill Meeting House. *I* think we should get married then! I've resigned my job here, effective the end of this month."

"I'm all for it, but that's only just over a month away. I don't see how it's possible," Adam protested.

"You, O mighty man of valor, are a famous railroad executive who can purchase a million dollars worth of track one week and have a thousand men working on it the next—yet you can't conceive of planning a wedding in five weeks? You seem to forget that I planned Emma Jane's and directed Mother's!"

"But . . . but, the invitations. I'm told that even here in Portland it may take a month to get them printed this time of year."

"Invitations, pish! You weren't listening. I said, 'Old Home Day'!"

"You mean?"

"Yes. Let's surprise 'em. The only ones who need to know are Mr. and Mrs. Baxter and the few who might not otherwise make it—I'll ask Emma Jane to be my matron of honor! There's dinner on the grounds planned right after church—a big picnic, and if it rains, it'll be in the grange hall next door. I shall have the wedding cake shipped over from Wareham, if I can get Emily Maxwell to agree to take charge of that little detail," Rebecca chortled.

"You *are* the executive, and you don't fool around when you make plans, do you?" Adam seemed immensely pleased. "But you'll forgive me—I've never been in a wedding before. What am *I* to do?"

"Be there, primarily, with two plain gold rings in your pocket. Wear a nice business suit—I don't want any silly silk hat and swallow-tail coat stuff. That's for poor bumpkins who want to show off or rich Bostonians who like to flash their money around," Rebecca said decidedly.

"There is one thing I can do. Have you planned the honeymoon yet?" Adam asked.

"Not unless we send Aunt Jane to Bermuda for a month so's we can have the brick house to ourselves undisturbed," said Rebecca. "That'd be honeymoon enough for me. And disconnect the phone. I don't want any of your junior executives phoning for advice."

"That won't be a problem."

"Why not?"

"Last week I submitted my resignation as CEO of the railroad, effective August first. The board of directors is right now looking for a replacement, though they do plan to continue with the program I've outlined for the next two years. Meanwhile, I'm seeking the Lord's will for a position in His service—perhaps running a home for homeless children or something like that."

"Adam!" Tears came to Rebecca's eyes as she spoke. "Oh, Adam, I'm so happy. I knew right along I wanted to marry you, but I was praying you'd seek to work with people in need. Now we can *truly* be one in heart."

"I've not forgotten what you said about making the brick house into a home for the homeless. But we can pursue that idea later. I believe I began to suggest an idea for the honeymoon."

"Yes?"

"How does Sunnybrook sound?" Adam inquired.

"Sunnybrook Farm? But I thought . . ."

"It'd be perfect. As a major company stockholder and former president, I won't have any trouble getting use of the place for a couple of weeks."

"But isn't construction going on there?" Rebecca asked.

"It's all done. As soon as the trestle is built across the gully south of Temperance the first train will run—right after Labor Day."

"What have you done with Sunnybrook Farm?"

"Of course you've seen the cemetery, when we went out there to bury Mark, a year ago," Adam told her.

"And the barn is gone, " said Rebecca.

"Where the barn stood is now a nice little stable for the stationmaster's driving horse and carriage. Where the tracks cross the road is a new loading platform for milk cans as well as a small depot and telegraph terminal."

"And the house—you promised you wouldn't tear our house down."

"Oh no! The house has a new roof, new porch, new paint, new wallpaper. It even has a bathroom with a big porcelain tub."

"But there's no running water," Rebecca objected.

"There is now—and 'city' pressure. We've put all copper pipes into the house and run a feed line from the new water tower installed to fill locomotives passing through. With five hundred gallons and a windmill on the well, the stationmaster's wife won't run out on laundry day, for sure."

"Stationmaster? Oh! There's a family living there?"

"Not until Labor Day weekend. The entire farm can be ours exclusively for the month of August, if we want it that long. I can have a rented horse and top-buggy left in the stable the day before the wedding, so we can have transportation all over Temperance and the countryside

Old Home Day at the Tory Hill Meeting House saw every seat filled.

around. And, hey! Here's a grand idea! There are about thirty miles of brand new track north of Temperance into Lewiston that won't have a train along until September. If I can borrow a handcar with a gas engine, we'll have our own private railroad. What do you say?"

"I say it sounds like fun," laughed Rebecca.

❧ ❧ ❧

Old Home Day at the Tory Hill Meeting House saw every seat filled. It was a marvelous August Sunday morning, and a Saturday night shower had left the air clean and fresh and, for early August, surprisingly cool.

Reverend Baxter was preaching on "Christ, the Head of the Home" that morning, and Rebecca, who had missed Sunday school and arrived late, was seated in a back pew with Mother, and Uncle Jerry Cobb; and with Will and Hannah, to whom Rebecca had sent a special invitation. Rebecca was pleased also to spy Adam's Aunt Mary Ladd seated near the front. Adam had brought his aunt in time for Sunday school, then explaining with a straight face that he'd been asked to entertain Rebecca for the afternoon, he had arranged for her to ride home with a neighbor.

Rebecca wore a new ankle-length dress of white cotton eyelet material with a silk petticoat underneath. White calfskin pumps tied with white ribbons, white silk hose, and white straw hat with a white satin bow sitting pertly atop her raven hair completed her wedding attire. Only a raspberry silk wrapper set off the white of her outfit. "Looks like you're gettin' ready for a weddin', Becky, darlin'," Aunt Jane had remarked earlier that morning as Rebecca was pressing the last wrinkle out of her new petticoat with a sadiron hot from the kitchen stove. Jane thought Rebecca's tastes in summer clothing rather extravagant, but unlike the departed Aunt Miranda, she tactfully kept her thoughts to herself.

When Adam, in the rig he usually rented from the Maplewood livery stable, stopped for Rebecca at a quarter to eleven, they had some discussion on whether they were actually going to pull this off. Most of Riverboro and North Riverboro were already at the meetinghouse, but all the same, the couple felt conspicuous indeed as they were eyed by the dozen or so stragglers who had missed Sunday school and who came only for the morning service. They were relieved, however, that no one seemed to notice when Adam and Rebecca drew into Cobb's drive and let John, who like his older sister had cut Sunday school that morning, hop in behind.

Adam drove directly to the meetinghouse's front steps, and passing the reins to John, he made a great show of elegantly handing Rebecca down and walking her to the foyer. He and John then parked the horse and wagon in the pine grove between the church and grange hall, as Rebecca squeezed into the back row, next to her mother.

The men lingered at the steps until the worshipers stood for the opening hymn, then they slipped into the vestry and quietly lifted two chairs into the foyer, sitting just outside the open double door to the sanctuary. Uncle Jerry, seeing John and Adam by themselves, slipped back and insisted, "You go 'n' sit with the women, Adam, seein's you're a visitor here. I'll stay back here with John."

"No, no, Uncle Jerry. I'm fine, right here. I've got to wait for a friend coming late," he said truthfully.

Aurelia, who had craned her neck to see what the fuss was about gasped, "Where did John get the new suit?"

"Adam bought it for him in Portland," Rebecca explained as quietly as she could. "John'll be a college sophomore this fall. We thought it was time he had a nice suit of clothes."

"We? Becky, you don't jest go askin' a gentleman friend to buy your brother new clothes."

"Please! It's all right Mother. Can we discuss it later?" This settled Aurelia for the time being, and mother and daughter joined the others in the final stanza of "The Church's One Foundation."

Halfway through the sermon, Adam, who had heard but little of Parson Baxter's discourse, rose from his chair. "C'mon, brother," he whispered, tugging John's sleeve. Walking quickly to where cakes and pies were spread on plank tables under the pines, Adam chose a spot where a clump of raspberry bushes hid the tables from view through the side windows of the church. He brought out a linen tablecloth that Rebecca had placed under the seat of the chaise, and he spread it out carefully.

Twice Adam paced the distance from the church to the picnic grounds. Times without number he anxiously checked his watch. Then "Here she comes," cried John, as Emily Maxwell turned her horse into the drive beyond the grange hall, made a wide swing through the pines, and pulled up by the tables. The wedding cake, at her feet in the buggy, was built on an oversize bread board. "I guess, Adam, you and Rebecca didn't reckon on how I'd get such a cake here from Wareham, traveling over gravel roads for an hour without having the frosting covered with dust."

Sheepishly, Adam confessed that they hadn't thought of that.

"Fortunately I was able to enlist some help." There sat the cake, encased in a cloth-covered pine box which, Adam later learned, had been constructed in haste the day before by an ingenious handyman on the custodial staff of Wareham Academy.

Quickly, carefully, he and John hoisted the cake onto the table, then with John at his heels, Adam made for the back door of the meetinghouse. Inside, they could hear the parson preaching as fervently as ever.

"Hey," John whispered, "I belong around front!"

"Where are the boutonnieres?" Adam exclaimed. He checked his watch. "Five minutes to go." Crouching low under the windows, he and John scooted around to the front entrance and entered as nonchalantly as they could. Fetching a shoe box from under the chair where he had been sitting, Adam, with John right behind him, ducked into the vestry.

Rebecca was there ahead of him, with Hannah and her new baby. Rebecca, her mothering instincts having taken over at an inopportune time, had made the mistake of picking the child up, and as infants will, it spit up. Frantically now, Hannah was trying to dry the mess with a clean diaper and baby powder.

Passing Rebecca her bouquet, Adam fished the boutonnieres out of the box, and soon they were pinned and ready. Adam opened the door. "I think that's our cue," he whispered, as Pastor Baxter remarked, "The members of the congregation will plcasc remain in their seats for a few moments after the benediction. We have a brief matter to attend to before we go into the grove for fellowship around the tables."

As the congregation bowed in prayer, Rebecca, suddenly composed and sure of herself, tiptoed to the door to the sanctuary. Gone was the raspberry shawl, and instead she wore a white veil. She clutched in both silk-gloved hands a large bouquet of daisies and black-eyed Susans.

Abijah and Emma Jane were seated down front, and Emma Jane, opening her eyes during the benediction, looked expectantly at Rebecca and smiled. She and Abijah were ready, Rebecca could see, to serve as matron of honor and best man.

Adam stepped up beside Rebecca and took her arm.

Two ten-year-old moppets, peeking around during the benediction, began to giggle uncontrollably.

John stepped right up behind Adam and tugged vigorously at his sleeve. "*I'm* the guy who walks the bride down the aisle, man. You go outside and 'round back, an' stand by the preacher when the organ starts to play. Use the back door."

Rebecca grinned in spite of herself. "Do what John says, dear," she murmured.

Rebecca's wedding was the talk of Riverboro for months to come. Only after the couple was installed in the brick house and it became apparent that Adam, who spent the fall months driving nails with the carpenters building a new dormitory for homeless children, was really an industrious individual, did the community forgive him for permitting Rebecca to arrange the surprise wedding. "Rebecca's allus bin a leetle mite crazy; I said so when she fust came here from Temp'rance," declared Mrs. Meserve. "That Adam Ladd, he's a good man, but if he lets her lead him into any more foolishness, their marriage won't last, mind ye."

Rebecca and Adam, for their part, had enjoyed their stay at Sunnybrook Farm while the tongues wagged in Riverboro. Sunnybrook was everything Adam had promised, and no happier bride on her honeymoon than Rebecca had ever vacationed in haunts so familiar yet so strange.

One spot however, Rebecca had avoided until the very last day before returning to Riverboro and the brick house. She and Adam had been for a swim in the pool beneath the willows and alders that once hid Rebecca's froggery, and they were now climbing the grade toward the Cape Cod cottage with its roof of new cedar on the slope above.

"Adam, when we drive the livery's rig over to Maplewood tomorrow, can we take the stagecoach the rest of the way into Riverboro? I'd like to return to the brick house just the way I first went there."

"I had planned on it," Adam assured her.

"I just wish that Uncle Jerry were still driving the stage," said Rebecca. "But, as you say, we grow up and we grow old. Each day unfolds to another until the Lord takes us home." Rebecca said no more as they walked on.

Pausing before an iron gate set in a rock wall under a wrought iron arch with the single word, "Sunnybrook," she placed her hand on the latch, opened it, then entered, as Adam followed close behind. She sat on the grass beneath a weeping willow and looked long and lovingly at three marble stones set there before a granite obelisk with the name "Randall" in relief letters. Rebecca wept silently as she viewed the latest grave, that of her youngest brother, Mark. Little Mira's headstone, she noticed, was etched with lichens; her father's even more so.

Rebecca ran her fingers across Lorenzo Randall's mossy stone. "If you can be as good a father to our children as Father was to us, Adam, I shall be supremely happy."

"We must go," she said at last, giving her hand to Adam. He smiled and helped her to her feet.

"Gravestones are really milestones," Rebecca remarked as Adam closed the gate behind them.

"How so?"

"Death is not an end; it is a beginning. I have had a new beginning today."

ABOUT THE AUTHOR

Eric E. Wiggin was born in 1939 in Albion, Maine, near where this story and its antecedents are set. His grandparents, with whom he shared his childhood, were contemporaries of Kate Douglas Wiggin. From them, from others of K.D.W.'s generation, and from his own experience he gleaned the background material for this novel.

The buck sheep story in chapter 12 is true; it was told Wiggin by a great-uncle, Oscar Bragg.

Wiggin now lives with his wife, Dorothy (nee Hackney), as a gentleman farmer near her childhood home in Fruitport, Michigan. The Wiggins are the parents of a girl and three boys, as well as three grandchildren. Wiggin has been a pastor, school teacher, and college instructor as well as a fish plant worker, news reporter, and editor.

The typeface for the text of this book is *Times Roman*. In 1930, typographer Stanley Morison joined the staff of *The Times* (London) to supervise design of a typeface for the reformatting of this renowned English daily. Morison had overseen type-library reforms at Cambridge University Press in 1925, but this new task would prove a formidable challenge despite a decade of experience in paleography, calligraphy, and typography. *Times New Roman* was credited as coming from Morison's original pencil renderings in the first years of the 1930s, but the typeface went through numerous changes under the scrutiny of a critical committee of dissatisfied *Times* staffers and editors. The resulting typeface, *Times Roman*, has been called the most used, most successful typeface of this century. The design is of enduring value to English and American printers and publishers, who choose the typeface for its readability and economy when run on today's high-speed presses.

Substantive Editing:
Michael S. Hyatt

Copy Editing:
Susan Kirby

Cover Design:
Steve Diggs & Friends
Nashville, Tennessee

Page Composition:
Xerox Ventura Publisher
Printware 720 IQ Laser Printer

Printing and Binding:
Maple-Vail Book Manufacturing Group,
York, Pennsylvania

Cover Printing:
Strine Printing
York, Pennsylvania